JESUS AND THE SWEET PILGRIM BAPTIST CHURCH

Jesus and the Sweet Pilgrim Baptist Church

A FABLE BY CLAYTON SULLIVAN

A Muscadine Book

University Press
of Mississippi
Jackson

www.upress.state.ms.us

First published in 1993 by Doubleday
Copyright © 2001 by Warren Clayton Sullivan
All rights reserved
Manufactured in the United States of America

06 05 04 03 02 01   4 3 2 1

The paper in this books meets the guidelines for perma-
nence and durability of the Committee on Production
Guidelines for Book Longevity of the Council on Library
Resources.

Library of Congress Cataloging-in-Publication Data

Sullivan, Clayton, 1930–
    Jesus and the Sweet Pilgrim Baptist Church : a fable /
by Clayton Sullivan.
        p. cm.
    "A muscadine book".
ISBN 1-57806-332-9 (alk. paper)
    1. Afro-American churches—Fiction. 2. Second
Advent—Fiction. 3. Jewish women—Fiction. 4.
Mississippi—Fiction. I. Title.

PS3569.U3465 J47 2001
813'.54—dc21

                                        00-049527

British Library Cataloging-in-Publication Data available

For Mae and Charlotte

Contents

ONE
Clearwater, Mississippi, 1964
11

TWO
The Announcement
13

THREE
The Coming
24

FOUR
Scissors, Toothpick, and Bigbottom
36

FIVE
Town Talk
46

Contents

SIX
Lulabell's Lounge
53

SEVEN
Sam Bernsteiner
63

EIGHT
The Sweet Pilgrim Field
72

NINE
The Metamorphosis
78

TEN
The Okatala Creek Bridge
84

ELEVEN
The Discovery
91

TWELVE
"They've Shot Jesus and Simon Peter!"
100

THIRTEEN
"When the Saints Go Marching In"
104

JESUS AND THE SWEET PILGRIM
BAPTIST CHURCH

ONE

Clearwater, Mississippi, 1964

WHAT FOLLOWS is an account of events which happened almost thirty years ago at the Sweet Pilgrim Baptist Church. This black congregation's house of worship —a rectangular, frame structure with a bell tower—is located two miles east of Clearwater, Naboshuba County's largest town and its county seat. To get to Clearwater you take Highway 47 southward out of Vicksburg. Twenty-one miles below Vicksburg you come to Clearwater, a three-traffic-light town straddling Highway 47, which goes on down to Natchez. With a population just over a thousand, it sits atop a bluff and overlooks the Mississippi River. From this bluff you can see the Mississippi for miles in both directions. At night —when a full moon is shining—the river looks like a silver necklace winding and twisting back and forth across the landscape. At the bottom of the bluff on which Clearwater sits there's a black settlement called Catfish Landing. Catfish Landing consists of tin-roofed shanties, river warehouses, and a honky-tonk named Lulabell's Lounge. From Catfish Landing a daytime ferry carries cars and trucks back and forth across the river to McKenzie, Louisiana.

Everyone concedes that curious events happened around Clearwater and in Naboshuba County during the spring and summer of 1964. But they have conflicting opinions about those episodes. Some Naboshuba County whites think deception was involved. Aware that blacks played pivotal roles, they quip, "There was a nigger in the woodpile somewhere." Other whites, although perplexed, are less skeptical. That's why they muse, "Some things happen in this world which we can't explain." All of Naboshuba County's blacks, however, are believers. They refer to the happenings which I'm about to relate as the "Sweet Pilgrim Miracle."

TWO

The Announcement

BELIEVERS IN THE MIRACLE agree it started at the Sweet Pilgrim Church's Easter service, and that it ended some six months later on the last Sunday in September —the day on which the Sweet Pilgrim Church always observed an annual homecoming. In 1964 Easter fell on March 29, and on that Easter Sunday evidences of spring's early arrival were everywhere. The woods around Clearwater sparkled with white dogwood. The azaleas—some red, some pink, others orange—were in bloom. Gum, hickory, and pecan trees had reclothed themselves with leaves. Oxeye daisies and black-eyed Susans were growing under fence rows and along road-sides. The sky, free of clouds, was as blue as Caribbean water, and the sun was beating down without mercy upon the one-room, frame building of the Sweet Pilgrim Baptist Church.

13

Jesus and the Sweet Pilgrim Baptist Church

The morning Easter service, led by Reverend Bob Stringer, was coming to a close. The congregation had sung the last song, and Brother Stringer was getting ready to pronounce the benediction. And then it happened. The Sweet Pilgrim Miracle began.

Far off in the distance—coming from the direction of the Mississippi River—celestial music was heard. Its melody suggested the hymn "Holy, Holy, Holy." The music's volume grew louder. Its source (whatever the source was) moved closer and closer to the Sweet Pilgrim Baptist Church. Finally, the awesome music engulfed the Sweet Pilgrim sanctuary. Some of the church members who were present that Easter morning said later that the music sounded to them like hundreds of organs being played simultaneously. Others suggested it sounded like a choir dominated by soprano voices and by church bells. Harvey Honea, who for years had worked as a janitor at the municipal auditorium in New Orleans, said the music sounded like a symphonic orchestra with thousands of instruments.

As the hauntingly beautiful music enveloped the Sweet Pilgrim congregation, its members became mesmerized. No one had sensations of fright or dread. Instead, everyone present experienced feelings of inner warmth and peace as the music flowed over and under and around the wooden church building.

After reaching a crescendo, the music momentarily subsided. Toward the front of the sanctuary a disembodied male voice spoke to the black parishioners. The message was succinct. The voice announced to the congregation: *"This coming Sunday, Jesus and Simon Peter will visit the Sweet Pilgrim Baptist Church."*

Those fourteen words constituted The Announcement. After these words had been uttered, the music momentarily grew louder but then subsided as its source slowly receded from the church toward the horizon, fading away across fields and woods in the direction of the Mississippi River.

After the music faded and could no longer be heard, the Easter-morning congregation at the Sweet Pilgrim Church sat stunned. For several minutes no one spoke. Or moved. No one looked either to the right or to the left. Instead, everyone's gaze was transfixed toward the front of the sanctuary where Brother Stringer, his mouth agape, was standing behind the pulpit.

Brother Stringer had the nickname of "Fishpole." He had been given this nickname because of his tall, erect body. Almost seven feet in height, Fishpole had his life turned topsy-turvy by the Second World War. Drafted in 1941, he was inducted into the army at Camp Shelby, the sprawling military base in the piney woods south of Hattiesburg. He went through basic training at Fort Knox in Kentucky and then was sent to Europe where he spent two years as an infantryman. While tramping across Germany through rain and snow, Fishpole experienced a "call" to preach. On returning to the States, he landed a job in Vicksburg with the post office. Six days a week Fishpole worked as a postman, trudging up and down Vicksburg's hilly streets delivering mail. But every Sunday he drove down to the Sweet Pilgrim community (where his mother, two sisters, and two brothers lived) to serve as the unpaid lay pastor of the Sweet Pilgrim Church.

The first person to break the silence which followed The Announcement was Aunt Mandy, the congregation's oldest and most respected member. In her youth Aunt Mandy had left the Sweet Pilgrim community to attend the Alcorn Agricultural and Mechanical College located only a few miles away in Lorman, Mississippi. Graduating from Alcorn, she attended Tuskegee Institute in Tuskegee, Alabama. Studying to be a teacher, Aunt Mandy put herself through these black schools. At Alcorn and at Tuskegee she "hired out to white folks" as a maid and domestic cook. She worked also as a café dishwasher. After graduating, Aunt Mandy returned to the Sweet Pilgrim community where for forty years she taught at the River Bluff School, Naboshuba County's segregated school for blacks. She ruled her elementary classes with an iron hand. A community saying was, "You give Aunt Mandy trouble and you've got trouble." Practically every member of the Sweet Pilgrim Baptist Church had been a student in her classes.

Aunt Mandy, now retired, her eyes covered with cataracts, was functionally blind. Over the years her cataractal eyes had become white like pearls. Sitting in the second pew from the front, she interrupted the silence which followed the celestial music by exclaiming, "Bless the Lord, O my soul, and forget not all His benefits! Again I say: Bless the Lord, O my soul!"

Slowly others began to speak. Speaking sporadically, they said: "O Lawd."

"Sweet Jesus."

"Amen!"

"Oh yes."

"Thank you, Lawd."

"Have mercy."

Both men and women took out handkerchiefs and wiped perspiration from their foreheads. Some women shed tears while others cooled their faces with cardboard fans which were portable advertisements for the Amazing Grace Funeral Home in Vicksburg.

Brother Stringer, standing behind the pulpit, finally spoke. Perplexed, gazing straight ahead, directing his remarks to his confounded parishioners, he stammered: "Brothers and sisters, I've heard *music* today. *Beautiful music!* And I heard a voice sayin' that next Sunday Jesus and Simon Peter are gonna visit the Sweet Pilgrim Baptist Church."

Aunt Mandy, her face and milky eyes shining, rejoined, "You *did,* Fishpole! That's *exactly* what you heard! *Jesus*—he's comin' with Simon Peter to the Sweet Pilgrim Church. They're comin' next Sunday!"

Other members joined in.

"I ain't *never* heard music like that music we just heard. *Never!*"

"Me neither!"

"Where'd that music come from?"

"It came down from heaven!"

"It sounded like angels singing. Hundreds of 'em singin' together!"

"Who was that voice sayin' that Jesus and Simon Peter are coming?"

"I don't know who it was, but that is *sho* what it said!"

These remarks having been uttered, a puzzled silence again descended upon the congregation. The Sweet Pilgrim membership was composed of three clans—the Honea family, the Brumfield family, and the Stringer family, from which Fishpole, the pastor, came. These names were remnants from the slave era. Prior to the Civil War thousands of acres of Naboshuba land had been purchased by Norman Honea, Alexander Brumfield, and Mason Stringer—three white Virginians who migrated to Mississippi in the 1820s. All three developed plantations. As slave owners, they gave their names to their slaves. Norman Honea, Alexander Brumfield, and Mason Stringer served in the Confederate Army and survived the siege of Vicksburg. After the war all three had deeded small land parcels to former slaves. This deeded land was the magnet which kept blacks in

Naboshuba County. A quid pro quo arrangement was worked out whereby liberated blacks, living on plots they now owned, farmed the landholdings of their former masters. The freed Honea, Brumfield, and Stringer slaves—transformed into sharecroppers—farmed on halves. This meant the land owners got half of what was raised while the sharecroppers kept the other half.

The years passed, and this sharecropper arrangement withered away with the disappearance of row-cropping. But the land remained. And so did the white and black descendants of Norman Honea, Alexander Brumfield, and Mason Stringer. Their white descendants ended up owning Clearwater's businesses and most of Naboshuba's land. Instead of raising cotton and corn, they grazed beef cattle, operated pulpwood yards and sawmills, and owned poultry farms on which they raised chickens by the hundreds of thousands. The Honea, Brumfield, and Stringer blacks no longer sharecropped. Instead, they labored on barges that floated up and down the Mississippi River, on poultry farms, and on rigs which drilled for oil in the shallow fields surrounding Natchez. Across the years they paid property taxes and held on for dear life to their land. They reasoned: "You can always get by if you have a few acres of land with a house to sleep in, a cow to milk, and a garden to raise collards and corn."

Over the years the Naboshuba land owned by blacks had been divided and then divided again as fathers and mothers died and deeded the land to sons and daughters. By fate these black landholdings were concentrated along the Okatala Creek, which flowed into the Mississippi River four miles south of Clearwater. In the middle of these landholdings stood the Sweet Pilgrim Baptist Church. The church's first structure had been a brush arbor built in the late 1860s by freed slaves. This brush arbor had been followed by a log-cabin church, which in turn was replaced by the present one-room, frame structure. Having a square bell tower, the house of worship was built during the early 1930s with lumber donated by the Crosby Lumber Company in Vicksburg. For decades (prior to telephones) the Sweet Pilgrim Church bell was the means by which the black community kept in touch. When someone died or got sick or when a house caught on fire, the church bell was rung. The bell's tolling aroused the community day or night. On hearing the bell's ringing, the blacks would ride on horseback to the church to find out who had died or was sick or what the emergency was.

The blanket of nonplussed silence which had again descended upon the Sweet Pilgrim congregation in the wake of The Announcement was lifted when Jasper Honea spoke. Jasper, porter and deliveryman for the White Dot Laundry and Cleaners on Main Street in Clearwater, leaned backward in his pew and said, "Fishpole, I can't deny what I've heard today anymore than I can deny my name's Jasper. But what are people who weren't here—who *didn't* hear the music and the voice—what are they gonna say when they hear about this? They're gonna say we're crazy. I can hear the white folks in town being smart aleck and sayin', 'Have you heard what the Sweet Pilgrim niggers said happened at the church Easter Sunday?' "

Miss Lucy, president of the Sweet Pilgrim Missionary Society, agreed. She said, "Jasper, I been sittin' here worryin' about the same thing. What we heard today was holy music and holy words, and I don't want nobody makin' light of it."

Addie Mae, Lucy's sister, stood and said, "I hears Jasper, and I hears Lucy. They's right. What's happened is holy and hard to believe. So I's got an idea: *Let's don't tell nobody!*"

A murmur of agreement erupted. Parishioners exclaimed:

"That's right, Addie Mae!"

"Ain't nobody else's business!"

"We don't want people snickering and makin' fun over what's happened."

"Folks who weren't here—I don't care whether they're white or black—they aren't gonna believe even if we told 'em."

Addie Mae continued. "And I got another suggestion. We want Jesus and Simon Peter to feel welcome when they come next Sunday. That's why I'm sayin' we oughta have a dinner-on-the-ground. *The biggest and the best dinner-on-the-ground the Sweet Pilgrim Church has ever had!* With fried chicken and tater salad and iced tea!"

Others joined in.

"Let's have banana puddin', too!"

"And homemade ice cream!"

Fishpole, an ear-to-ear smile on his face, rapped the pulpit with his knuckles. He affirmed, "Addie Mae, you've come up with just what we oughta do. Let's keep what's happened this morning—I'm talkin' about the music and the voice—let's keep it to ourselves. And then next Sunday let's have a dinner-on-the-ground for Jesus and Simon Peter!"

A sense of excitement permeated the sanctuary. Everyone started speaking.

"I'm all for it!"

"Dinner-on-the-ground for Jesus and Simon Peter!"

"That's what we're gonna do!"

"Amen!"

Fishpole brought the congregation back to order. Again rapping the pulpit with his knuckles, he said, "I want all of you to look me square in the eye and answer this question: *How many of you promise you aren't gonna say a word to anybody about what's happened here today?* Lift your hand up high."

Everyone in the congregation raised a hand.

Fishpole continued. "All right, I've got another question. *How many of you promise you'll be here next Sunday?* Lift your hand up high."

Again every person raised a hand. Fishpole responded: "That's fine. Real fine. We're gonna keep what's happened today strictly among ourselves, and next Sunday we're gonna break bread together with Jesus and Simon Peter."

Fishpole, clearing his throat, pulled out his Hamilton pocket watch. Looking at the watch, he said, "It's almost one o'clock. We're goin', but before we go I want us to lift a prayer to heaven."

The men got on their knees. Every head was bowed. Then Fishpole prayed:

O Lawd, our Lawd, you have been in this place today. This morning we've heard music the likes of which we never heard before. And we've heard words spoken we never expected to hear. We want you to know we're grateful for all that's happened. And we're looking forward to next Sunday when Jesus and Simon Peter will be comin' here to the Sweet Pilgrim Baptist Church. Help us to prepare for their coming. Amen and amen.

And the parishioners said, "Amen!"

THREE

The Coming

MONDAY, Tuesday, Wednesday, and Thursday passed. Not a member of the Sweet Pilgrim Church broke the secrecy pledge. Although they discussed the celestial music and the puzzling announcement about Jesus and Simon Peter among themselves, they did not breathe a word about either to outsiders.

On Friday morning, Fishpole had his best suit—a black, pin-striped Hart, Schaffner, and Marx suit with vest and narrow lapels—cleaned and pressed. Miss Lucy and Addie Mae, sisters, drove up to Vicksburg and bought new hats at Fred's Discount Store. On Friday afternoon, Moses Stringer, towboat cook and father of six, drove his family over to Jackson and outfitted his three daughters and three sons with new suits and dresses purchased at a Kmart store.

On Saturday morning, the members gathered to clean

the Sweet Pilgrim Church and to groom the grounds. The women swept the sanctuary floor, washed windows, and dusted pews and pulpit furniture. The men mowed the grass, raked the yard, and with hammers and nails repaired the wooden tables (positioned under two oaks on the church's south side) upon which dinners-on-the-ground were always served.

When Sunday morning arrived, all members of the Sweet Pilgrim Baptist Church were out of bed by sunrise, preparing food for the dinner-on-the-ground for Jesus and Simon Peter. Miss Lucy, missionary society president, had organized the dinner-on-the-ground down to the last napkin, fork, and spoon. She'd appointed Bessie Stringer head of the fried chicken committee. Hattie Mae Brumfield was put in charge of vegetables and potato salad. Arlena Honea was assigned responsibility for rolls and desserts (banana pudding and homemade ice cream). Eloise Brumfield was given the task of securing paper goods (napkins, plates, cups, plastic forks and spoons). She was also responsible for iced tea. Miss Lucy had told Jason Honea to make sure there was ample ice. To that end, Jason had bought three stainless steel washtubs at the Western Auto Store in Clearwater. Early Sunday morning, he drove his Ford pickup to Stogner's Grocery and purchased thirty bags of crushed ice. He brought them to the church and packed them under sawdust in the newly purchased tubs.

By nine o'clock on Sunday morning parishioners began arriving at the Sweet Pilgrim Church. All were dressed in their Sunday best. As families arrived, they placed dishes of food (cloth-covered to foil insects) on the wooden tables, which were shaded from the sun by water oaks.

By ten o'clock, all members of the Sweet Pilgrim Church had arrived. With a sense of expectation, they assembled in the sanctuary. Fishpole, his shoes shined like glass marbles, began the service with prayer. Then the congregation, standing and singing with fervor, sang, "When We Walk with the Lord." And while the congregation was singing the third stanza The Coming occurred. The Sweet Pilgrim congregational singing was at first supplemented but was then supplanted by cosmic music—the same music which the previous Sunday had transfixed the congregation. Again—coming from the direction of the Mississippi River—angelic music was heard. Growing ever louder, it moved closer and then engulfed the austere Sweet Pilgrim sanctuary. Hauntingly beautiful, the music again flowed through, over, under, and around the wooden structure. The music, awesome and comforting, gripped the congregants who listened with reverence and joy.

As the music reached a climax, the sanctuary began filling with a white cloud. The cloud mysteriously emerged out of the sanctuary floor and billowed upward to the ceiling. It flowed over the parishioners like morning fog. Toward the front of the church the cloud thickened, becoming so intense that Fishpole and the pulpit were no longer visible to the congregation. This synthesis of music and cloud was an overwhelming aesthetic experience.

But then the music began to fade and the cloud began to lift, like haze evaporating in sunlight. The thinning cloud disclosed two persons materializing before the congregation. The materializing figures, who were at the front of the sanctuary next to Fishpole, became firmer and more distinct. All eyes of the Sweet Pilgrim congregation were riveted on the two people who appeared as the cloud vaporized.

Smiling, the person standing next to Fishpole looked at the nonplussed parishioners and said, "Good morning!"

There was no response. Unmoving, mute, staring like mannequins with human eyes, the congregants pondered the two figures who had emerged from the cloud and were now standing before them. The members of the Sweet Pilgrim congregation were too awed or confused to respond. Their sense of puzzled awe arose from the uniqueness and unexpectedness of what had happened. All week long the congregants, looking forward to Jesus' and Simon Peter's arrival, had been expecting male visitors. But the two persons who emerged out of the cloud were *women*. With Semitic facial features and coal-black hair, attractive in appearance, they were dressed like Fifth Avenue fashion models.

The prolonged silence was broken when the figure who had said "Good morning!" turned toward the pastor and asked, "Fishpole, won't you or one of your parishioners say something?"

Stammering, Fishpole responded, "Pardon me, miss, but *who are you*?"

"I'm Jesus."

A murmur, half-suppressed, rolled over the congregation.

"And this person standing beside me is Simon Peter."

Simon Peter smiled and nodded her head toward the congregants.

Again a perplexed murmur reverberated through the audience.

Fishpole, speaking haltingly, said, "Jesus, we were all lookin' forward to you and Simon Peter comin' and visitin' us today. But we were expectin' you to be *men*."

Jesus answered, "At times, Fishpole, I've come to earth in the form of a man. But this time I've come as a woman. Is something wrong with me appearing as a woman?"

Fishpole hastily said, "No! There's nothing wrong with it. It's just that—like I said—we all thought you were gonna be a man. And we thought Simon Peter was gonna be a man, too. You caught us by surprise."

Jesus and Simon Peter chuckled.

28

Jesus said, "We'll discuss this male-female issue some other time. Simply let me say that the two of us are glad to be with you today. And while we're briefly here we want to be sources of consolation. That's why I'm very anxious to meet Aunt Mandy. Aunt Mandy, where are you?"

Aunt Mandy, speaking with exhilaration, said, *"Here I am,* Miss Jesus."

Aunt Mandy, her body bent with age, her eyes blinded by cataracts, stood.

Jesus said, "Aunt Mandy, I want you to come down here to the front where Peter, Fishpole, and I are."

Aunt Mandy responded, "Miss Jesus, *I'm comin'.* I sho' am. I'm comin' *right now*!"

Aunt Mandy emerged from behind the second pew and with halting steps, tapping her way with a cane, walked to where Jesus was standing.

Jesus put her arms around Aunt Mandy's shoulders. She asked rhetorically, "Aunt Mandy, you can't see, can you?"

Her voice quivering, Aunt Mandy said, "No, Miss Jesus, I can't. Haven't seen for years. These cataracts—they've done me in."

Compassionately, Jesus said, "I understand."

Aunt Mandy aimlessly said, "I haven't really seen since my husband died. That was ten years ago."

Jesus said, "I understand."

Jesus reached out and put her hands over Aunt

29

Mandy's eyes. Then looking upward toward the sanctuary's ceiling, Jesus pronounced, "Through the power of God, maker of heaven and earth, I restore to you—Aunt Mandy—your sight. To God be the glory!" These words Jesus spoke authoritatively.

With the uttering of those words Aunt Mandy's cataracts disappeared.

A startled expression came over Aunt Mandy's face. Jubilantly, she exclaimed, "O Lawd! O Jesus, *I can see! I ain't seen for years. But now I can see! I see Fishpole! I see the church house!"*

Whirling around, lifting her arms, smiling exuberantly, Aunt Mandy exploded, *"And I see all the members of the Sweet Pilgrim Baptist Church!"*

A wave of wonder swept over the congregation. Everyone stood. They started clapping and shouting.

"Hallelujah!"

"Thank you, Jesus!"

"Praise the Lord!"

The clapping and the adulatory exclamations rocked the sanctuary. They continued until Jesus put her finger to her mouth, indicating a desire for silence. The congregation quieted instantly.

Jesus said, "Aunt Mandy, I want you to stay here beside me. *Now—where's Tadpole?"*

"Tadpole" was the nickname of Elijah Honea. Twelve years old, he was Jason Honea's youngest son. Elijah was nicknamed "Tadpole" because of his diminutive size. Weighing a hundred pounds, Tadpole had been born with a clubfoot. This misshapen limb necessitated his wearing on his right foot a specially designed shoe. The shoe had an elevated sole which was four inches thick. Tadpole had limped from birth, and the spectacle of his hobbling to school and limping down Clearwater's Main Street was a familiar sight to Naboshuba County residents.

Responding to Jesus' inquiry about Tadpole, a chorus of voices exclaimed, "Tadpole's in the back!"

All members of the congregation turned in Tadpole's direction. Some pointed fingers at him.

They said, "That's Tadpole—the little fellow in the white suit!"

Jesus said, "Tadpole, I want you to come down here where I am."

The congregants advised, "You heard what Jesus said, Tadpole. You get yoself down there *right now*!"

Tadpole, dressed in a tight-fitting cotton suit and leaning on his crutch, hobbled to the front where Jesus, Simon Peter, Aunt Mandy, and Fishpole were standing. Jesus reached out and drew Tadpole closely to her. Tadpole, overwhelmed by what was happening, looked at the floor.

Jesus remarked, "Tadpole, don't look downward. Look at me. Look into my face."

Tadpole, saying nothing, responded to Jesus' request.

Jesus continued, "Tadpole, it's been hard being crippled, hasn't it?"

Tadpole moved his head up and down, signaling a positive response.

Looking into the youngster's eyes, Jesus asked, "Would you like to be healed?"

A gasp of anticipation swept over the Sweet Pilgrim congregants. Tadpole moved his head upward and downward, vigorously indicating a positive response to Jesus' inquiry.

Jesus, speaking with authority, looking upward, said, "Tadpole, I now command that your clubfoot be made whole through the power of God—maker of heaven and earth!"

A nondescript noise reverberated through the church. Some who witnessed Tadpole's healing said later it sounded like the cracking of a whip or the firing of a gun. The noise startled everyone.

Tadpole collapsed to the floor and started shouting, *"Sumpin'* is *happenin'* to me! *Sumpin'* is happenin'!"

All eyes were riveted on Tadpole as he shouted and rolled on the floor.

Jesus interrupted Tadpole's shouting. She said, "Tadpole, take your right shoe off!"

Tadpole's response was, "I'm shakin' too much to take my shoe off. I'm flitterin' all over!"

Jesus turned toward Moses Stringer and Isaiah Brumfield—two muscular men who worked on river barges and who were standing beside the piano. Pointing toward Moses and Isaiah, Jesus said, "I want you two fellows to help Tadpole take his shoe off."

Quickly Moses and Isaiah walked over and knelt beside Tadpole. Restraining Tadpole with his hands, Moses urged, "Tadpole, you be still. You stop this shakin' so Isaiah and me can take yo shoe off."

Isaiah and Moses untied the laces on Tadpole's right shoe and slipped it off the previously deformed foot. They also removed Tadpole's left shoe.

Jesus instructed Moses and Isaiah, "Help Tadpole stand up."

Moses and Isaiah put their hands under Tadpole's arms and lifted him to his feet.

Jesus said, "Tadpole, look at your right foot."

As Tadpole looked downward, Jesus continued, "See, it's straight. It's normal. And your right leg is longer now. It's the same length as your left leg. That's why I want you to walk without your crutch."

Tadpole responded, "Miss Jesus, I ain't sure I can. I's always walked with a crutch."

Jesus answered, "If you believe you can walk without a crutch, Tadpole, you can."

Members of the congregation responded. *"Believe, Tadpole! Believe what Jesus is sayin'!"*

Silence gripped the congregation. All eyes were focused on Tadpole. Tadpole took one step without his crutch. Then another step. And another and another.

Aunt Mandy exclaimed, "Tadpole, honey child, you're *walkin'*! You're walkin' without a crutch!"

With jubilation, Tadpole exploded, "I can't believe it! My right leg is as long as my left leg! And my clubfoot is straight and I's walkin'!"

Congregants joined Tadpole in his jubilation.

"Praise be to God!"

"Tadpole's done been healed!"

"Tadpole's walkin'!"

"Hallelujah and thank you, Jesus!"

Tadpole, gaining confidence, walked around the piano. Then he walked up and down the center aisle.

The congregants, watching with astonishment, broke into applause. They began clapping and rhythmically chanting, *"Run,* Tadpole, *run! Run,* Tadpole, *run!"*

Responding to the chants, Tadpole started galloping back and forth between the pulpit and the rear of the church.

In the midst of the rhythmic chanting and clapping, Henrietta Honea, pianist for the Sweet Pilgrim Church, walked over and sat down at the upright Baldwin piano. For twenty-two years she had been church pianist, and in the course of those years she had learned all the hymns and spirituals in the Sweet Pilgrim repertoire by heart. While playing the piano she always closed her eyes and swayed her body from side to side.

With eyes closed, with body swaying, with a confident keyboard touch, Henrietta spontaneously started playing the Joseph Scriven hymn, "What a Friend We Have in Jesus." Hearing the music, the congregation began singing with gusto:

> What a friend we have in Jesus
> All our sins and griefs to bear!
> What a privilege to carry
> Everything to God in prayer!
> O, what peace . . .

FOUR

Scissors, Toothpick, and Bigbottom

THIS LADEN-WITH-EMOTION singing was interrupted by the staccato sounding of a car horn. Stirring up a dust cloud, a battered, red Ford sedan—with horn blaring—came down the road and pulled up in front of the Sweet Pilgrim Church. Painted on both sides (in gold and black letters) were the words: THE LOLLIPOP RAGTIME BAND.

Three corpulent, laughing black men, dressed in white suits, piled out. They were Alex and Sidney and Roger Brumfield. Born and reared in the Sweet Pilgrim community, cousins to one another, they lived and worked in New Orleans. All three had nicknames which had displaced their given names. Alex was known by everyone as "Scissors." Endowed with a sense of humor, he acquired "Scissors" for a nickname because (so everyone said) he was always "cutting up." Sidney was called "Toothpick" because when a youngster he always had a toothpick in his mouth. Roger had acquired "Bigbottom" for a nickname because of his corpulent size. Sidney and Roger worked for the New Orleans sanitation department. Alex drove a bus for the municipal transit system. First as a hobby, then as a means of supplementing their incomes, Scissors, Toothpick, and Bigbottom had organized the Lollipop Ragtime Band. Scissors played trumpet, Toothpick played trombone, and Bigbottom played banjo. They performed at weddings and dances. On Friday and Saturday nights they played and tap-danced at the Cajun Corner, a black nightclub on the edge of the French Quarter. Periodically Scissors, Toothpick, and Bigbottom drove up from New Orleans to spend Sundays with their Sweet Pilgrim relatives.

Having rolled out of the Ford sedan, Scissors, Toothpick, and Bigbottom ran up the steps and walked into the church. The hymn singing abruptly stopped. The members of the congregation turned and faced the rear where Scissors, Toothpick, and Bigbottom were standing. Giggling, extending his arms, Scissors announced:

I WANT EVERYBODY HERE TO GIVE ME YO EAR!
WE TAPDANCING LOLLIPOPS—WE'RE ALL THREE
HERE!

Scissors, Toothpick, and Bigbottom broke out into guffaws.

No person in the Sweet Pilgrim congregation laughed. Everyone silently and disapprovingly stared at the white-suited threesome.

Miss Lucy, missionary society president, and Addie Mae, Miss Lucy's sister, had the custom of bringing umbrellas to church. Spring, summer, fall, or winter, rain or shine, hot or cold, all fifty-two Sundays in the year, they brought umbrellas to the morning worship service. Grabbing their umbrellas, Miss Lucy and Addie Mae stepped out of their pew and walked to the rear of the sanctuary. Without saying a word, obviously vexed, they started raining blows on Scissors', Toothpick's, and Bigbottom's heads.

Surprised and puzzled, Scissors, Toothpick, and Bigbottom tried to dodge the umbrella assault. They emitted yelps of pain.

Covering his head with his hands and arms, Scissors exclaimed, "Miss Lucy, what's wrong? What are you mad about?"

Miss Lucy snapped, "Scissors, you and Toothpick and Bigbottom oughta be *ashamed* of yoself."

Scissors responded, "We're just havin' a little fun."

Toothpick joined in, "We thought we'd spice up Fishpole's sermon."

Addie Mae opined, "You boys been drinkin'. I smell whiskey."

Bigbottom confessed, "We're drinkin' but we ain't drinkin' all that much."

Miss Lucy retorted, "You three oughta be whipped! Whipped like mules! Comin' into the church horsin' around when we got visitors. Special visitors!"

Scissors responded, "Special visitors? Who's visitin'?"

Addie Mae answered, "The two ladies at the front."

Scissors, Toothpick, and Bigbottom looked toward the front of the sanctuary where Jesus and Simon Peter in female form were standing beside Fishpole.

Bigbottom inquired, "Them two ladies at the front?"

Toothpick, perplexed, asked, "Who is they?"

Miss Lucy answered, "That's Jesus and Simon Peter."

Scissors, Toothpick, and Bigbottom looked at the two female figures. They then looked at one another. For a second time all three bent over and broke out into guffaws.

Again they were bombarded with swinging umbrella blows by Miss Lucy and Addie Mae. Scissors, Toothpick, and Bigbottom crouched over, avoiding the blows as best they could.

Aunt Mandy, her vision restored, intervened. Walking down the aisle to where the umbrella bombardment was taking place, she commanded, "Lucy, you and Addie Mae stop hittin' these boys!"

With an authoritarian voice that recalled the way she once quieted unruly students, Aunt Mandy continued. "Scissors, Lucy's right. You three straighten up and straighten up right now! Something wonderful has happened here today."

Miss Lucy and Addie Mae stopped their umbrella battering. Scissors, Toothpick, and Bigbottom rose from crouched to upright postures.

Toothpick, straightening his coat and tie, asked, "What's happened, Aunt Mandy?"

Aunt Mandy replied, "You boys look straight at me. What's different about me today and the way I was the last time you saw me?"

Puzzled, looking at Aunt Mandy, Toothpick observed, "Sumpin' is different, Aunt Mandy. Ain't no doubt about that."

"Look at my eyes."

Looking closely, Bigbottom exploded, "I got it! *Yo cataracts is gone!*"

Aunt Mandy rejoined, "They sure are. Guess what happened to 'em?"

Bigbottom retorted, "What?"

Aunt Mandy replied, "A few moments ago Jesus commanded them to go away and away they went. I can see now. Today is the first time I've seen for years."

Scissors, Toothpick, and Bigbottom exchanged perplexed looks.

Aunt Mandy added, "And look what Jesus did for Tadpole. Tadpole—you come here!" Tadpole walked to where the Lollipops were standing.

Aunt Mandy instructed, "Look at Tadpole's foot and

leg. His foot's been healed and his right leg is now as long as his left leg. And he's walkin' without his crutch. Jesus healed Tadpole."

Looking at Tadpole, Aunt Mandy continued, "Tadpole, walk some so Scissors, Toothpick, and Bigbottom can see what I'm talkin' about."

Dressed in his sockfeet, Tadpole marched down the aisle toward the front where Fishpole, Jesus, and Simon Peter were standing. Scissors, Toothpick, and Bigbottom —along with Aunt Mandy, Miss Lucy, and Addie Mae— followed. The Lollipops stared at Tadpole as he walked. No one said a word. So quiet was the congregation one could have heard a feather fall.

Arriving at the sanctuary's front, Scissors stammered, "I've known Tadpole from the day he was born. I know he's always been lame with a clubfoot. I see him healed and walkin'. And here's Aunt Mandy with her cataracts gone. Tadpole walkin' and Aunt Mandy seein' I can't deny."

Turning toward Jesus and Simon Peter, speaking softly, Scissors continued, "And I see these two lovely visitors. I'm told by Aunt Mandy you're Jesus and Simon Peter. Now may the good Lord in heaven above forgive me for sayin' what I'm about to say, but I'll say it anyway. I've always thought Jesus and Simon Peter were men. Yet you two are women. So how can you be Jesus and Simon Peter?"

Jesus answered, "At times, Scissors, I've come to

41

earth as a man. This time, however, I'm appearing before the Sweet Pilgrim Church as a woman. It's that simple."

As Jesus was speaking Bigbottom crumpled to his knees and collapsed face forward on the floor.

Aunt Mandy exclaimed, "Bigbottom's fainted!"

Voices from the congregation spoke up.

"Get some water!"

"And ice!"

"A towel, too!"

Bessie Stringer, Arlena Honea, and Isaiah Brumfield scampered out of the church to get water, ice, and a towel.

Fishpole and Scissors rolled Bigbottom over on his back. Toothpick took off his coat, folded it into a pillow, and placed it under Bigbottom's head.

Fishpole ordered, "Let's all stand back. Bigbottom needs air."

Bessie and Arlena, returning with a pan of water, knelt beside Bigbottom. They started wiping and fanning his face.

Speaking gently, Bessie said, "Everything's all right, Bigbottom. Don't you be afraid."

Fishpole barked, "Bigbottom, can you hear me? Come to, Bigbottom! You done fainted!"

Bigbottom, moaning, moved his head from side to side. He muttered, "O Lord, have mercy. It's too heavy to handle."

42

Fishpole helped Bigbottom rise to a sitting position.

Bigbottom muttered, "I'm sorry. I didn't mean to faint."

Bessie said, "That's okay, Bigbottom, don't be ashamed."

Scissors responded, "Come to think of it, I feel a little woozy, too. To drive up and come in the church and be told that Jesus and Simon Peter are here. Like Bigbottom says, it's too heavy to handle."

Toothpick added, "It's heavier than heavy."

Aunt Mandy observed, "There's no need to say it's heavy. There's no need to be afraid. Scissors, you and Toothpick and Bigbottom look around. None of us are afraid. None of us are rattled. Are we? The reason you three are rattled is because you didn't hear the music when Jesus and Simon Peter came."

Members of the congregation agreed. They said:

"That's right!"

"You didn't hear the music!"

Aunt Mandy explained, "When Jesus and Simon Peter came this morning they were accompanied by music from heaven. Wonderful music . . . beautiful music that made you feel good on the inside and at peace with the world. That's why we aren't scared."

Tadpole said, "Aunt Mandy's right. Us who heard the music ain't scared. We's *happy*. Why, I'm so happy I could dance."

43

Jesus asked, "Tadpole, why don't you? I'd love to see you dance."

Tadpole responded, "Miss Jesus, I ain't never danced before. Up to now I've been crippled, and crippled folks don't dance."

Scissors interrupted, "Fiddle, Tadpole, we've got all kinds of tap shoes out in the car. I'll get you a pair of tap shoes and you're gonna dance. I'll show you how. You're gonna dance for Jesus and Simon Peter to the music of the Lollipop Ragtime Band!"

Exhilarated, Scissors, Toothpick, and Bigbottom ran out of the sanctuary. From the trunk of their red Ford they removed a trumpet, a trombone, a banjo, and several pairs of tap-dancing shoes. They rushed back into the sanctuary. Finding a pair that fit Tadpole, Scissors helped him put them on.

Also slipping into tap-dancing shoes, Scissors said, "Tadpole, you watch me and do like I do."

Toothpick on trombone and Bigbottom on banjo began playing "When the Saints Go Marching In." Scissors started tap-dancing, and Tadpole imitated the steps.

At first Tadpole's dancing was tentative and halting. But then it became more vigorous. And still more energetic.

The Sweet Pilgrim congregation broke out in laughter and applause as Tadpole danced beside, behind, and in front of the pulpit. Scissors—on trumpet—joined Toothpick and Bigbottom in their ragtime playing.

The music of the Lollipops was soon complemented by cosmic music—the same music which earlier that morning had filled the sanctuary. Its melody too was "When the Saints Go Marching In." Immediately after the cosmic music filled the sanctuary, the mysterious cloud reappeared, rising again out of the floor. The cloud was as thick as river fog. In the midst of the cloud the people laughed and clapped, Tadpole vigorously danced, and the Lollipops enthusiastically played. But then suddenly the cosmic music faded. And the cloud evaporated. Fishpole, the Lollipops, and the members of the Sweet Pilgrim Church looked around for Jesus and Simon Peter. Jesus and Simon Peter had vanished with the cloud.

FIVE

Town Talk

THREE-TRAFFIC-LIGHT Mississippi towns are extended families. Everyone, black and white, knows everyone else. There are no strangers. Instead, each resident knows everyone else's age, parentage, income, residence, and place of employment.

Thus in Clearwater Aunt Mandy was a familiar figure. For decades she had been a schoolteacher. She shopped weekly at Oliver Stogner's grocery, Clearwater's major food store. Aunt Mandy's husband had been killed in a train accident. That she received a $75,000 damage settlement from the Illinois Central Railroad was common knowledge around Clearwater. And that she had deposited this money on interest in the Naboshuba Farmers' Bank was also common knowledge. People remarked, "You know, just to look at Aunt Mandy, the way she dresses and the way she lives, you'd never know she was sittin' on that kind of money." More than one Naboshuba black had tried to borrow money from her. But her standard response was, "The good Lord has told me not to lend to anybody."

With the double onslaught of age and cataracts, Aunt Mandy had retired from teaching. She lived off modest state retirement and Social Security payments and off interest from the Illinois Central Railroad settlement.

Tadpole, likewise, was a Naboshuba institution. Jason Honea, his father, was school janitor. When people thought about Tadpole they thought about peanuts. Known around Clearwater as the "peanut boy," Tadpole every Saturday sold peanuts (parched and bagged by his mother on Friday nights) to passersby on Main Street. Farmers ate Tadpole's peanuts as they sat on the courthouse steps and talked about politics and the weather. The spectacle of Tadpole, born deformed, pulling around the courthouse square a red wagon filled with bagged peanuts was as familiar to Naboshuba residents as the spectacle of dusty roads in August.

Aunt Mandy's sight recovery, Tadpole's healing, and the (alleged) Jesus-and-Peter appearance became Clearwater's conversation topic par excellence. Although some suggested fraud, no one could deny that Aunt Mandy (without a cataract operation) was seeing again and that Tadpole was walking normally.

Oliver Stogner, owner of Stogner's Grocery, articulated the puzzlement shared by Naboshuba whites. He remarked, "Last Saturday Aunt Mandy came into the store blind as a bat . . . the way she's been comin' into my store for years. She bought a quart of buttermilk, a can of sardines, and a box of crackers. I know what I'm talkin' about because I waited on her myself. Then Monday morning she came into the store as spry as a chicken and seein' as good as I can. And no sooner had Aunt Mandy walked in than into the store walks Tadpole. I've known that little nigger all his life. I couldn't count the times he's hobbled into my store to buy a root beer. But in he comes walking without a crutch and minus his clubfoot. I swear to God, you could have knocked me over with a flea."

The Sit and Sip Bridge Club always met on Tuesday afternoons. The four ladies composing the Sit and Sip Bridge Club were the cream of Clearwater's aristocracy. They were Odessa Brumfield, Sarah Ann Honea, Betty Stringer, and Frances Pigott. Lamar Brumfield, Odessa's husband, was president of the Naboshuba Farmers' Bank. Hank Honea, Sarah Ann's husband, owned the Naboshuba Chevrolet Company. Betty's husband was Dr. Samuel Stringer, Clearwater's leading physician. Buddy Pigott, Frances's husband, was a pharmacist and owner of the Friendly Neighbor Drugstore.

The Sit and Sip Bridge Club always began playing promptly at two o'clock and played bridge until the sun went down. During the course of these weekly gatherings, Odessa, Sarah Ann, Betty, and Frances variously sipped coffee, tea, hot chocolate, rum-'n'-Cokes, along with gin-'n'-tonics. And during the course of these weekly gatherings (which had been held regularly for twenty-two years except when Christmas or Christmas Eve fell on Tuesdays), they analyzed and dissected whatever happened to be the subject of current interest in Clearwater.

Not surprisingly, the bridge club discussion that second Tuesday after Easter was consumed with what supposedly had happened out at the *nigger* church.

Bessie, Frances Pigott's maid, was a Sweet Pilgrim member. Frances, holding cards in one hand and coffee in the other, recounted, "When I got wind of it I went to the kitchen and I said to Bessie, 'Now, Bessie, I want you and me to sit down right here at this table, and I want you to tell me about what happened last Sunday at the Sweet Pilgrim Church.' And Bessie—speaking in her drawl—said, 'Well, Miss Frances, I'll tell you, but you ain't gonna believe me. All I can say is, may the good Lord strike me dead if I ain't tellin' the truth.' And then Bessie launched into this *bizarre* story about how on Easter Sunday their church was filled with music and how a voice announced that Jesus would come the next Sunday. Bessie then said that last Sunday, day before yesterday, the music came again and that Jesus came out of a cloud and healed Aunt Mandy and Tadpole, the peanut boy. The strangest thing of all was Bessie saying that Simon Peter came with Jesus and that both were women."

Sarah Ann interjected, "That's what all the niggers are saying."

Betty remarked, "I don't believe it. I don't believe a word of it."

Frances rejoined, "I don't want to believe it either. But Bessie told me all this with a straight face. I can tell when Bessie is out-and-out lying. And so help me, she didn't sound like she was lying."

Odessa inquired, "Have any of you seen either Aunt Mandy or the little Honea nigger since this happened?"

Sarah Ann answered, "I haven't, but Hank has. Jason, Tadpole's daddy, drives a Chevrolet truck, and Hank vows that yesterday Jason came to the shop to get a new muffler and had Tadpole with him. Hank made it a point to get a good look at Tadpole's right leg, and he tells me it's as sound as a silver dollar."

Odessa said, "I'll be damn! That's unbelievable! I've seen that little nigger walking around on a shriveled leg all his life."

Frances remarked, "The whole thing is a puzzle. I talked to Oliver this morning at the grocery, and he assures me *something* has happened. *Exactly what* he doesn't know. But what he *does* know is that both Aunt Mandy and Tadpole have been in his store since Sunday. Aunt Mandy's cataracts are gone, Tadpole is walking, and both say Jesus, looking like a woman, cured them at the Sweet Pilgrim Church."

Odessa said, "That gives me the creeps." Frances, Betty, and Sarah Ann rejoined, "Me, too!"

Whereupon Odessa proposed they momentarily stop playing bridge and mix gin-'n'-tonics to calm their nerves. This they did.

The Sweet Pilgrim issue was discussed at the Wednesday night prayer meeting of Clearwater's First Baptist Church. The First Baptist Church, most prominent church in Naboshuba County, was pastored by the Reverend Wally Criswell, graduate of the Great Western Baptist Theological Seminary in Dallas. Brother Criswell took pride in his fundamentalism. Time and again he told his admiring parishioners, "If it's in the Bible, I believe it; if it's contrary to the Bible, I don't believe it."

Thus when Miss Elvira McDonald stood in prayer meeting and asked, "Brother Criswell, what do you think about what the niggers are saying happened last Sunday at the Sweet Pilgrim Church?" he had a ready answer. His response was: "I don't believe there's anything to it, and I'll tell you why I feel that way. What the niggers are saying happened can't be harmonized with the Bible. The Bible *does* predict Jesus is coming again. But it says he'll descend from heaven with a shout, with the archangel, and with the trumpet of God, and it says that when Jesus comes, the dead will be raised. Now I ask you: Did any of these things happen last Sunday?

51

Did the trumpet sound? Were the dead raised? Did the archangel come? You know the answer as well as I do. The answer is *No!* I'm of the opinion that the whole thing is some kind of hoax. Or maybe it's the work of the devil."

Miss Elvira said, "You may be right, preacher, but Tadpole walking sure makes me wonder."

Always permeated with profanity and cigar smoke, its walls plastered with girlie calendars, Clawd Fiker's Pool Hall was Clearwater's redneck hangout—a place respectable people avoided. Its owner spelled his first name "Clawd," not "Claude." He did this because his bucolic mother had written "Clawd" on his birth certificate and in the family Bible. At this pool hall the Sweet Pilgrim miracle was treated with jest. Clawd Fiker, farting as he talked, remarked, "The whole thing's a crock of bullshit. What tickles me is the way them niggers got so excited they ran off and forgot their goddamn dinner-on-the-ground."

SIX

Lulabell's Lounge

PLASTERED with Philip Morris, Budweiser, Barq's Root Beer, and Coca-Cola advertisements, Lulabell's Lounge was Naboshuba County's black hangout. On weekends cars by the dozens encircled this frame, tin-roofed structure where blacks gathered to drink beer, to eat barbecue, to gossip, and to play cards. A saying around Clearwater was, "A nigger can get anything he wants at Lulabell's Lounge." By "anything" was meant gambling, food, beer, wine, whiskey, sex, companionship. Located in Catfish Landing at the base of the vertical cliff on which Clearwater was situated, Lulabell's Lounge was one place Naboshuba blacks had to themselves. The only whites who ever walked through its doors were salesmen who came weekly (usually on Monday) to take orders for food, paper, and beverage supplies.

Lulabell's Lounge was owned and operated by Chester Travis, a muscular fellow who resembled a bald-headed, Japanese wrestler dyed black. A native of Naboshuba County, he had run away as a young man to join the United States Merchant Marine. For twenty years he sailed around the world—to England, to Australia, to Japan, to Brazil. After twenty years in the Merchant Marine, Chester returned to Clearwater and established Lulabell's Lounge where he ran a tight ship. No customer "messed around" with Chester. People quipped, "Mess around with Chester and he'll beat your tail off."

On Thursday night following the Sunday on which Jesus and Simon Peter appeared at the Sweet Pilgrim Church, a thunderstorm drenched Clearwater and Naboshuba County. The storm, charged with thunder and lightning, moved in from the west between seven and eight o'clock, soon after nightfall. Rain poured down in sheets, and the shanties in Catfish Landing resembled houseboats as rainwater flowed beneath and around them.

Thursday night was traditionally a slow night at Lulabell's Lounge. As Chester Travis (the composite owner, operator, cook, bartender, janitor, and bouncer) expressed it: "Business on Thursday night is always slower than molasses on a cold day in January." Because of the rainstorm, business was particularly slow that Thursday night in April. Only two customers were present. One was Rosco Jones, who drove a tractor-pulled mower for the Mississippi Highway Department. The second customer was Moses Stringer. Moses worked out of Vicksburg on a river barge and had been present the preceding Sunday at the Sweet Pilgrim Church when the puzzling visitation had taken place.

The three men were sitting around a table in the middle of the honky-tonk. Each man was leisurely puffing a cigar.

Chester, his bald head reflecting the light bulb above the table, and Rosco were listening to Moses. Moses—as he talked—rocked back and forth in a cane-bottom chair. He had a faraway look in his eyes.

Moses said, "I know there's something to it. Your own eyes and ears don't lie to you. I was there *both* Sundays. Sunday before last—Easter Sunday—and then last Sunday. On Easter Sunday the church filled with music. A voice came out of the music sayin' that the next Sunday Jesus and Simon Peter was comin'. Then last Sunday the music and a cloud came. And out of the cloud came these two women sayin' they was Jesus and Simon Peter. The lady who said she was Jesus cured Aunt Mandy's cataracts, and then she cured Tadpole. Tadpole got to rollin' on the floor, shakin' like a leaf. Jesus told me and Isaiah to hold him down and take his shoes off—which we did. Right there before my eyes Tadpole's leg and foot straightened out. And the funny thing is it all seemed natural. Nobody was scared. The whole thing was peaceful, giving you a good feeling on the inside."

Chester, blowing a ring with cigar smoke, said, "Wished I'd been there."

Rosco agreed, "Me, too."

Chester inquired, "Why didn't you spread the word about what was gonna happen? Then we all coulda been there."

Moses responded, "We was afraid people would laugh and make fun. So we decided to keep it to ourselves. That way nobody could dump on it."

Chester asked, "What did Jesus and Simon Peter look like?"

Moses answered, "Real nice looking . . . sharp . . . high class. Nothing cheap about 'em. They looked like Jewish ladies—dark eyes, black hair. You could tell they both had been around. Believe you me, they was in charge. When Jesus said 'Hop,' we hopped."

Chuckling, Rosco said, "I bet you did."

Chester remarked, "This whole thing has shook everybody up. It's all us black folks are talkin' about, and it's all the white folks are talkin' about. They can't explain it. They particularly can't explain Tadpole. Aunt Mandy they could explain. Maybe she had a cataract operation. But Tadpole—there ain't no explaining him. He was hobbling on Saturday and walking right on Monday. That nobody can deny."

The most elegant item in Lulabell's Lounge was a

grandfather's clock which Chester had purchased years before from Hudson's Bankrupt Store in Hattiesburg. The mahogany clock sat incongruously beside the lounge's multicolored, illuminated jukebox. The clock began striking ten, and, while the tenth hour was being chimed, a vehicle pulled up to the lounge and parked at the front entrance. Since the lounge's door was open, the vehicle's arrival was heard by Chester, Moses, and Rosco.

Chester mused, "Who could that be comin' in here this time of night?"

The sound of car doors slamming was heard.

Chester, Moses, and Rosco—puffing on their cigars—looked toward the door.

Into Lulabell's Lounge stepped two stylishly dressed women. They were the same two who the preceding Sunday had materialized out of the cloud at the Sweet Pilgrim Baptist Church.

Chester, Moses, and Rosco sat stunned. Staring at the women, unable to speak or to move, they resembled three stones. Moments of awkward, puzzled silence passed.

Finally Jesus, smiling, spoke. "Hello, Chester; hello, Moses; and hello, Rosco."

Moses, stammering, said, "Chester, I want you and Rosco to believe me. These two ladies are the ladies who visited our church last Sunday. This is Jesus and Simon Peter."

Chester stood and walked slowly toward the entrance where Jesus and Simon Peter were standing. Speaking softly, extending his arms, he said, "Miss Jesus, I see you know my name. It's Chester . . . Chester Travis. I want to welcome you and Simon Peter to Lulabell's Lounge. You comin' here tonight is the greatest thing that has ever happened in my life."

Jesus answered, "Chester, you're kind to say that. We're honored to be with you."

Chester inquired, "Won't you and Simon Peter come on in and sit down with us?"

Jesus and Simon Peter responded, "We'll be glad to."

Rosco, who had risen to his feet, pulled up two additional chairs to the table. He—motioning with his hand —said, "Now, Miss Jesus, you sit here. And Miss Simon Peter, you sit right here."

Chester, obviously excited, asked, "Can I get you something? Maybe something to drink?"

Jesus answered, "Of course. How about a glass of white wine?"

Simon Peter joined in, "Me, too."

Chester responded, "Yes, indeed! Two glasses of Chablis comin' up!"

Chester scampered behind the bar. Having filled two wineglasses, he returned to the table and placed the Chablis before Jesus and Simon Peter.

Jesus and Simon Peter, speaking simultaneously, said, "Thank you."

Chester answered, "You're welcome, you're very welcome."

Muttering to himself, Chester continued, "This I can't believe . . . Jesus and Simon Peter turning up out of a thunderstorm at Lulabell's Lounge . . . I can't believe it."

Outside, the rain continued falling lightly. The thunder rumbling became more distant. Jesus, Simon Peter, Chester, Rosco, and Moses carried on a rollicking conversation—a discussion which lasted two hours. They talked about George Wallace and Ross Barnett, Alabama's and Mississippi's controversial politicians. They discussed Martin Luther King and what he was up to. They talked about how Naboshuba Countians were "all shook up" over what had happened to Aunt Mandy and to Tadpole and about how people were nonplussed over Jesus' and Simon Peter's reappearance as women. Throughout the conversation Chester, Rosco, and Moses—experiencing a quiet, inner joy—were as relaxed as dozing bird dogs.

The grandfather's clock struck twelve o'clock.

After the twelfth chime was sounded, Jesus looked at Moses and inquired, "Moses, suppose your relatives and friends out in the Sweet Pilgrim community were asked, 'What do you need to make your life in Naboshuba County better?' If asked that question, what would they say?"

Moses, without hesitation, said, "Better ways to make

a living . . . more ways to be *on our own* . . . more ways to put money in our pockets.''

Rosco joined in, ''We black folks needs to be independent, not always being on Mr. Charley's payroll.''

Moses continued, ''The white folks own Naboshuba County—most of the land, the sawmills, the wood yards, the poultry sheds, and the businesses on Main Street. We 'niggers' live on the edges. Me—I'm a deckhand on a barge. Seven days on, seven days off, and always one paycheck from being broke. You ask me what we blacks want? Well, that's my answer . . . to feel you aren't always on the verge of going broke . . . to get ahead so life can be better.''

Chester broke in, ''Moses, he is singin' on key tonight.''

Rosco said, ''Amen!''

Moses added, ''When you're shut out, it does something to you. Makes you angry and numb on the inside. Not being able to provide for your family the way you want to.''

For several moments no one spoke a word.

Finally, Jesus broke the silence. ''Moses, a week from now a man named Sam Bernsteiner is going to come to Clearwater. Sam Bernsteiner from Longview, Texas. He is a man to be trusted. I want you to tell the folks in the Sweet Pilgrim community to do what Mr. Bernsteiner suggests.''

Moses inquired, "What's he gonna suggest?"

Jesus responded, "I'd rather not say. Just remember the name—Sam Bernsteiner. He'll be a short man with tan skin—skin brown as leather from being in the sun. And he'll have gray hair. This Sunday tell the folks at the Sweet Pilgrim Church to cooperate with Mr. Bernsteiner. If they don't, we'll all be sorry."

Having spoken these words, Jesus abruptly stood. So did Simon Peter. They bade Chester, Moses, and Rosco good night.

Perplexed over the references to a Mr. Bernsteiner, the three black men accompanied Jesus and Simon Peter to the door.

On reaching the door, Jesus said, "Chester, I've got one request to make. Don't tell anyone about my being here tonight. Tell the people out in the Sweet Pilgrim community that the person who advised you about Mr. Bernsteiner wants to remain unknown. In other words, let's keep this meeting here tonight among ourselves." The three men shook their heads affirmatively.

Jesus and Simon Peter walked out of Lulabell's Lounge accompanied by Chester, Moses, and Rosco. The rain had stopped, and the sky was fair. Jesus and Simon Peter got into a red Jeep. Painted on both sides (in black) was a Star of David, an emblem visible because of the exterior neon lights of Lulabell's Lounge and an emblem Chester, Moses, and Rosco looked at but did not comprehend. They watched as the Jeep wound its way up the serpentine road which led from Catfish Landing to the top of the bluff. The Jeep reached the bluff's top. Its rear lights merged into the lights of Clearwater.

SEVEN

Sam Bernsteiner

THE MORNING coffee regulars at the Top-of-the-Bluff Café, Clearwater's main restaurant, remembered precisely when Sam Bernsteiner arrived in town. He arrived on April 23, a Thursday. On that Thursday morning, Edgar Pittman (retired school principal), Andy Estess (retired county agent), and Jeffrey Stogner (retired postmaster) were sitting at the café's front table from which they had a clear view of the courthouse square. Drinking coffee together, engaging in small talk, they saw a stately, black automobile pull into a parking space directly in front of the Top-of-the-Bluff Café. From the car emerged a stocky man with gray hair. He was wearing denim pants, a denim shirt, and brown boots. About him was an "I-don't-have-any-time-to-waste" air. He walked to the trunk of his car, opened it, and removed a briefcase. Having locked the trunk, he headed across the street toward the courthouse.

Edgar, watching the stranger's every move, asked, "Who do you suppose he is?"

Jeffrey responded, "Damn if I know. Never saw him before."

Andy inquired, "What kind of car is that?"

Jeffrey answered, "Damn if I know that either. I've never seen a car like that."

Edgar commented, "Looks to me like a foreign car."

The denim-clad stranger, his head bent toward the ground, disappeared across the street into the courthouse.

Jeffrey said, "You fellows keep your seat. I'm gonna go out there and find out what kinda car that is."

Jeffrey got up from the table and walked out onto the sidewalk. He made a reconnaissance of the limousine, walking around it twice, noting its Texas license plate.

Returning to the restaurant, Jeffrey boomed, "I want everybody here to know that parked outside this café is a black, high-class Rolls-Royce from Texas!"

Peggy Sue, a bantam waitress with red hair, responded, "Jeffrey Stogner, you're puttin' us on."

Jeffrey answered, "Naugh, I'm not. Go out there and look for yourself. If that's not a Rolls-Royce from Texas, I'll eat my shoe."

Curiosity-filled, Peggy Sue walked out on the street. Like a dog sniffing a bone, she surveyed the car. She cupped her hands to her eyes and peered inside. She wrote down on her order pad the license number.

Walking back inside the restaurant, Peggy Sue announced, "I'm here—like Jeffrey—to tell you that parked out in front of the Top-of-the-Bluff Café in Clearwater, Mississippi, is a black, four-door Rolls-Royce with leather seats and with the fanciest dashboard you ever seen and with Texas license plate SB264-618!"

Looking up from the grill where he was scrambling eggs, Buck Lowe—the café's owner—drawled, "What-do-ya-spose-at-fella's-doin'-here-in-Clearwater?"

Small towns in Mississippi have no secrets. The community grapevine discovers and communicates all. This person talks to that person who shares what another person said. Thus, by three o'clock Thursday afternoon the following facts were well known in Clearwater:

The man who had arrived in town driving a Rolls-Royce was named Sam Bernsteiner.

Sam Bernsteiner was an independent oil driller from Longview, Texas.

His Rolls-Royce cost between $75,000 and $100,000. This automotive tidbit had been unearthed by Hank Honea, owner of the Naboshuba Chevrolet Company.

Sam Bernsteiner was registered at the Holiday Inn in Vicksburg.

He had eaten his noon meal at the Top-of-the-Bluff Café. Instead of sitting at a table, he had sat at the counter. He had complimented the roast beef ("The tenderest I've ever eaten") and had left Peggy Sue a ten-dollar tip. Peggy Sue reported this tip to all the café's regular patrons. In reporting this tip, she said, "I've waited on tables in this café for twenty-four years, and this is the *first time anybody* has *ever* tipped me ten dollars. I tell you right now—this fellow from Texas has class. Real class. I wish my everyday customers had class and tipped the way this Mr. Bernsteiner does. The trouble is—the regulars around here are so tight-fisted they think they're tippin' big if they leave a quarter."

Also by three o'clock on Thursday afternoon the business community in Clearwater had learned that Sam Bernsteiner was a heavyweight in the oil business. This insight was the result of a phone call made by Lamar Brumfield, president of the Naboshuba Farmers' Bank. He made a long-distance call to the Deposit Guaranty Bank of Jackson and asked Martin Dedeaux, head of the bank's oil and gas division, to use his contacts in Texas to check out one Sam Bernsteiner from Longview. Mr. Dedeaux contacted a banking colleague in Longview who informed him that Sam Bernsteiner was an eccentric, bachelor Jew who was well known around Longview and was "sharper than an ice pick" when it came to drilling for oil. Indeed, the banking source in Longview told Mr. Dedeaux that Sam Bernsteiner could drill producing oil wells as readily as a "farmer could find hens in a henhouse." This information Mr. Dedeaux relayed back to Lamar Brumfield in Clearwater.

Thus of no small interest to everyone in Clearwater was what Sam Bernsteiner did that Thursday morning when he walked into the chancery clerk's office, which was located on the first floor of the courthouse. He asked to speak to Denver Honea, chancery clerk. He introduced himself ("Mr. Honea, my name's Sam Bernsteiner. I'm from Longview, Texas, and I'm in the oil business") and told the chancery clerk he wanted to gather information concerning land ownership in Sections 25 through 27 and Sections 34 through 36 of Township Three East. These sections, two miles wide and three miles long, through which the Okatala Creek ran, formed the heart of the Sweet Pilgrim community.

Sitting in a corner at an oaken table used by lawyers to do legal research, perusing land deed records, scribbling on note cards and legal pads, consulting repeatedly a map provided by the chancery clerk, Mr. Bernsteiner wrote down with meticulous care landowners' names and legal descriptions of their property.

He spent all day Thursday and Friday doing title research in the chancery clerk's office. When time came Friday afternoon to close down for the weekend, Mr. Bernsteiner said to the three women who worked in the office, "Ladies, I've gathered all the deed information I need. The three of you have been courteous and helpful and I want you to know I appreciate it." Whereupon he presented each with a box of chocolate-covered almonds and Scotch-taped to each box was a crisp hundred-dollar bill. They squealed with delight, planted kisses on Mr. Bernsteiner's forehead, and told him to drop by the office any time he needed additional title information.

Mr. Bernsteiner spent Friday night at Vicksburg's Holiday Inn. Early Saturday morning, still wearing boots, still dressed in a denim shirt and denim pants, he started going from house to house in the Sweet Pilgrim community. His approach was forthright. Mr. Bernsteiner didn't dilly-dally. Walking up to a black home, he would knock on the front door and ask to speak to the owner. His unvarying explanation was, "A good day to you, my name's Sam Bernsteiner, and I'm from Longview, Texas. I'm with the Big B Oil Company, and we're thinking about drilling for oil here in Naboshuba County. I'd like to talk with you about leasing your land."

The blacks he visited that Saturday were receptive. Such was the case because the previous Sunday (April 19) Chester Travis, owner of Lulabell's Lounge, Rosco Jones, and Moses Stringer made it a point to attend the morning worship service at the Sweet Pilgrim Church. After the worship service they circulated among the parishioners and mentioned the possibility of a Mr. Bernsteiner turning up, and that if he did turn up, they ought to pay attention to what this man from Longview, Texas, had to say. People asked them, "How come you know about this man?'' They answered enigmatically, ''Just take our word for it.''

News of Mr. Bernsteiner and what he was up to (''He says they gonna drill for oil!'' ''He'll pay you money to lease your land!'') spread like a grass fire through the Sweet Pilgrim community. Instead of Mr. Bernsteiner continuing to go to blacks, they started coming to him. He set up shop at the Sweet Pilgrim Church. For two days, landowners bringing deeds as evidence of ownership came to him. Sitting at one of the tables used for dinners-on-the-ground, Mr. Bernsteiner filled out leasing forms and issued lease checks. He leased land belonging to Aunt Mandy, to Brother Stringer, to Miss Lucy and her sister Addie Mae, and to Jasper Honea, the White Dot Laundry's deliveryman. Contacted by telephone, Alex and Sidney and Roger Brumfield (the Lollipop Ragtime Band trio) drove up from New Orleans and signed leases. Indeed, by week's end, Mr. Bernsteiner had leased every land parcel owned by the black Honea, Stringer, and Brumfield clans of the Sweet Pilgrim community.

After this leasing marathon, Mr. Bernsteiner disappeared from Naboshuba County. He checked out of the Holiday Inn in Vicksburg and returned to Texas. A week passed. Another week passed. Then on the third Monday in May, as Sid Stringer, one of Clearwater's policemen, expressed it, ''All hell broke loose.'' That Monday morning huge trucks with Texas license plates came rolling into Clearwater. Not one truck, but a caravan. Not Fords and Chevrolets, but Diamond Ts and Peterbilts. They were driven by bearded Texans, wearing sunglasses, and they were loaded with bulldozers, oil rigs, drilling pipe, metal tool sheds, and diesel generators. Painted apple green, they had signs painted on their doors which read: THE BIG B DRILLING COMPANY, LONGVIEW, TEXAS.

Their arrival in Clearwater created interest like a circus parade. The coffee regulars at the Top-of-the-Bluff Café got up from their tables and walked out on the street. Gaping, they asked, "What in the devil is going on?"

Mr. Bernsteiner, driving his elegant, black Rolls-Royce, arrived with the caravan. Mr. Bernsteiner and the apple green trucks drove through Clearwater and headed toward the Sweet Pilgrim community. Several trucks ended up at Jasper Honea's farm; others ended up at Roger Brumfield's place. Yellow bulldozers were unloaded and operators started grading rig sites. When nightfall came, the site preparation did not stop. It did not stop because the Big B Drilling Company had diesel generators which provided electricity for banks of lights —lights suggestive of stadium lights used to illuminate football fields for night games. Consequently, the crews, working in shifts, operated around the clock. Two rigs, both over a hundred feet in height, were assembled. The tool pushers and roughnecks started drilling.

At night the rigs, from a distance looking like illuminated trees, were visible from Clearwater. During both day and night people came from all parts of Naboshuba County to watch them. They learned to distinguish between the sound the rigs made when drilling and the sound they made when pulling pipe.

Rig workers drove into Clearwater to buy supplies (food, gasoline, diesel fuel). People asked, "How's it looking?" "How deep do you fellas plan to drill?" "Have you found anything yet?" Workers responded, "We're paid to keep our mouths shut."

Mr. Bernsteiner drove into town every day to eat his noon meal at the Top-of-the-Bluff Café. While eating one of his noon meals, he was approached by Mike Aycock, Farm Bureau Insurance agent and owner of eighty acres immediately south of the Sweet Pilgrim community. He asked the Texan if he would be interested in leasing his eighty acres. Responding politely, Mr. Bernsteiner said, "Mike, I appreciate the offer. But right now I've leased all the land I can say grace over."

EIGHT

The Sweet Pilgrim Field

IN 1964 THE MONTH of May had five Sundays. On the evening of the fifth Sunday (May 31), Lamar Brumfield, president of the Naboshuba Farmers' Bank, was absorbed in his hobby: broiling steaks and shrimp-wrapped-in-bacon-strips over a charcoal fire. Lamar and Odessa, his wife, had invited over Hank and Sarah Ann Honea, Betty and Sam Stringer, and Frances and Buddy Pigott (the four wives constituting the Sit and Sip Bridge Club). These four couples, Clearwater's social and financial elite, were sitting on the Brumfields' patio. The men were drinking Manhattans, while discussing a proposed strip shopping center on the south side of town. Their wives were working out details of a projected trip in Betty Stringer's new Lincoln Continental to New Orleans to dine at Commander's Palace.

The patio phone rang.

Lamar, tongs in hand, perspiration on his forehead, his attention focused on the charbroiling steaks and shrimp, said, "Don't answer it. Let it go."

The phone's ringing stopped. A moment of silence followed. And then the phone started ringing again.

Lamar, with disgust, said, "Damn Alexander Graham Bell and all telephones everywhere."

Odessa responded, "I'd better answer it."

She picked up the receiver and said, "Hello." She listened intently. Then turning to her husband, Odessa said, "Lamar, it's long distance. You'd better take it. The man—whoever he is—says he *must* speak to you."

Lamar, handing the tongs to his wife, took the receiver in hand and said, "Hello, this is Lamar Brumfield."

For several moments, Lamar listened without saying a word. And then he interjected, "I'll be damn."

As the one-sided conversation continued, Lamar—with rising excitement in his voice—said time and again, "I'll be damn."

Hank, Sam, and Buddy stopped talking. So did their wives. Obviously, they intuited, Lamar was being told significant news.

Lamar's final remark over the phone was, "Martin, I appreciate this information. I *mean* I appreciate it. I'll get right on top of this and see what can be done. Maybe we'll all end up being as rich as the Hunts in Dallas or the Basses in Fort Worth."

Putting down the receiver, a look of wonder on his face, Lamar said, "That was Martin Dedeaux, one of the oil-and-gas boys with the Deposit Guaranty Bank in Jackson. Weeks ago, I called and asked him to check out Sam Bernsteiner, that oddball Jew from Texas who's drillin' those two wells out at Sweet Pilgrim. Fifteen minutes ago he got a call from an oil buddy of his out in Longview, and this friend told him they've hit oil in both of those Sweet Pilgrim wells. In *both* of 'em! They're double-deckers. They hit Wilcox sand at 5,000 feet, and they hit Tuscaloosa around 10,000 feet. How thick the sands are he doesn't know. But they must be deep because the Big B Oil Company has six more rigs on the way from Longview. They're supposed to roll in here tonight."

Hank, Sam, and Buddy came to attention.

Buddy exploded, "Damn it! Last year I had a chance to buy a hundred acres out there for a song, and I let the chance go by. I could kick myself in my big, fat ass."

Sam inquired, "How much acreage did Bernsteiner lease out there?"

Lamar replied, "The chancery clerk's office tells me he's locked up every square inch in the Sweet Pilgrim community. He's leased heavily in Sections 25, 26, and 27 and in Sections 34, 35, and 36."

Sam moaned, "We've all sat on our fannies, twiddled our thumbs, done nothing, and now we've let this cow-boy from Texas come in here—into our backyard—and drill two oil wells under our noses."

Hank rejoined, "I didn't sit on my fanny. When I got wind of what Bernsteiner was up to, me and Ralph Bain drove up to Jackson and talked to some oil people up there. We talked to the Moungers and to the Campbells and to a fellow named Frascogna. All of 'em told us there was no way in God's good name to bring in a producing oil well where Bernsteiner was drilling. They had dozens of fancy maps and geological charts— which meant nothing to me—but they took 'em all down and got out their pens and pencils and explained —like Moses explaining the Ten Commandments—why Bernsteiner was making a fool of himself and was throwing away his money like a boozed-up sailor on a weekend pass."

By Monday afternoon (June 1) news of the Sweet Pilgrim oil discovery was known all over Naboshuba County. People could talk about nothing else. By Tuesday afternoon everyone knew:

That six additional rigs from Longview had arrived late Sunday night. These rigs were being assembled to drill more wells in the Sweet Pilgrim field.

That the chancery clerk's office was running over with lease hounds from Jackson, New Orleans, Shreveport, Longview, Tyler, and Dallas.

That land close to the Sweet Pilgrim field was leasing for thousands of dollars per acre.

That representatives from the Texaco Oil Company had rented an office over Buddy Pigott's drugstore.

That every room at the Pink Shutters, Clearwater's only motel, was rented out to oil people. Virginia Lowrie, motel manager, affirmed this was the first time in her memory when *all* her rooms were rented.

That the Top-of-the-Bluff Café was hiring an additional cook and two more waitresses to take care of increased business.

That Jasper Honea, the White Dot Laundry's janitor and deliveryman on whose land the first well was drilled, had walked into the Clearwater National Bank with a check for twenty-five thousand drawn on an account of the Big B Oil Company in Longview. Jasper asked for the twenty-five thousand in fifty- and hundred-dollar bills. These bills, the tellers related, he placed in an empty molasses can, which he tucked under his arm as he walked out. The coffee regulars at the Top-of-the-Bluff Café said they were going to buy shovels and go out every night to Jasper's farm and dig until they found that molasses can.

The air over Clearwater and Naboshuba County became permeated with oil-boom fever. Every person who owned an acre of ground in Naboshuba County dreamed of wealth. Not of minuscule wealth, but of extravagant wealth.

Land owned by whites located in proximity to the Sweet Pilgrim field was leased by competing oil companies: by the Anderson and Anderson Drilling Company in Shreveport, by the Blue Star Production Company out of Tyler, and by the Bellweather Corporation from Dallas.

At the height of Naboshuba's oil boom twenty rigs were drilling simultaneously. People quipped, "At night Naboshuba County looks like a lit-up pinball machine." During the day Clearwater's courthouse square was clogged with cars of out-of-town lawyers, lease hounds, and curiosity seekers. All available rooms in private homes were rented out. The Top-of-the-Bluff Café, for the first time since it opened its doors in 1942, operated around the clock. Denver Honea, chancery clerk, kept his courthouse office open on weekday nights until eight. The Sunday edition of Jackson's *Clarion Ledger,* Mississippi's largest newspaper, carried a front-page story entitled, "SPECTACULAR OIL FIELD DEVELOPING IN NABOSHUBA COUNTY." The story's subtitle affirmed: "FIELD TO BE CALLED THE SWEET PILGRIM FIELD." Members of the Clearwater Rotary Club toyed with the possibility of forming a locally owned drilling company.

NINE

The Metamorphosis

BUT BY THE END of July a metamorphosis in attitude had taken place among Naboshuba County whites. Their attitude about the oil boom went from excitement to perplexity and from jealousy to anger and hostility. This attitudinal change was due to the course the oil boom took. Without exception, all wells drilled by Sam Bernsteiner in the Sweet Pilgrim community came in gushers. Every well was a double-decker, pumping from Wilcox and Tuscaloosa sands. In total, thirty-eight producing wells were brought in. Circular, steel tanks were erected in which to store the extracted oil. The oil was then transferred from these facilities into tanker trucks which hauled it down to Catfish Landing. There it was pumped into barges which floated the oil downriver to refineries in Baton Rouge.

Yet every well drilled on white-owned property—

even on land located adjacent to the Sweet Pilgrim field —came in as a dry hole.

People said, "This is crazy. It makes no sense at all. Drill on nigger land and in comes a gusher. But drill on white property and all you get is a headache and a hole in the ground."

One by one oil men from Tyler and Dallas and Shreveport folded their rigs and left Naboshuba County. Befuddled, sadder, wiser, these departing oil men said, "We've taken a hit." Pointing toward the ground, they also said, "We can't figure out what's down there. How can you have such thick producing sands in a circumscribed area like the Sweet Pilgrim field? Sam Bernsteiner drills and brings in a producer; we offset two inches from his well and bring in a dry hole. We've never seen anything like it."

Naboshuba whites began boiling with jealousy. Stories circulated around the courthouse and on Main Street about blacks cashing royalty checks at the Clearwater National Bank—checks for $3,000 and $9,000 and $16,000. With this money they were buying new Buicks and John Deere tractors and Ford pickups. Fishpole, the preacher, purchased a Cadillac sedan in Vicksburg.

Hank Honea, owner of the Naboshuba Chevrolet Company, observed, "For years and years the best I could do was sell dilapidated, used cars on credit to the blacks out in the Sweet Pilgrim settlement. Now they've got money, and instead of buying new Chevrolets from me, they go up to Vicksburg and pay cash for Buicks and Cadillacs."

Several blacks receiving monthly royalty checks ("More money than we knowed was in the world") quit their jobs at sawmills and poultry farms and on river barges. White employers complained, "Hell, it's gettin' to the place where you can't get a Sweet Pilgrim nigger to work no more." Housewives opined, "There's not a black woman in Naboshuba County you can hire to be a maid."

Contemptuous jests abounded. "I hear every grocery store in town is doin' a land-office business in chitlins and pigs' feet. They can't keep 'em in stock."

Others said, "It's like Bilbo predicted. The alleys are takin' over the avenues."

Most outraged were the redneck regulars at Clawd Fiker's Pool Hall. Three regular customers were Roger and Alex Rainey and Barney Fiker, Clawd's brother.

Roger, Alex, and Barney—like Clawd—despised the oil boom that had befallen the Sweet Pilgrim community. They said, "Them niggers don't need that kinda money."

The day was Saturday, the month was August, the time was eight o'clock at night. Roger, Alex, and Barney were drinking beer in Clawd's pool hall.

While pouring beer into a frosted glass, Alex opined, "The world's goin' to hell in a handbasket. You can see it in the way the niggers are rollin' in money from them oil wells. All they do now is sit on their black asses and cash them big royalty checks."

Leaning behind the bar, a cigar in his hand, Clawd said, "The time's comin' when ever' nigger in Naboshuba County is gonna be drivin' a Cadillac . . . like Fishpole, the damn nigger preacher."

Alex continued, "And the world's goin' to hell in a handbasket 'cause ever' time you turn on your TV all you hear about is them civil rights workers from up North comin' down here and tellin' the niggers they're as good as white people . . . tryin' to get 'em to vote and to sit with white folks. I believe them nuns and rabbis oughta go back to Boston and work on their own problems instead of comin' down here and givin' us hell. If the Yankees want to mix with the niggers, that's fine. But don't make us mix with the darkies if we don't want to."

Clawd, puffing on his cigar, observed, "None of them nigger-lovin' civil rights workers better turn up in Naboshuba County. We'll bust their butts."

Barney responded, "We've already got 'em—right here in Naboshuba County."

Clawd said, "Like hell we have."

Barney insisted, "We *do* have some."

Clawd quipped, "You're full of crap."

Barney continued, "You shoulda been out at the sale barn this morning. Three different people—Sam Porter,

Rayford Pigott, and Earl McDonald—told about seein' a Jeep runnin' around the county with two women in it. Two white women. Sam and Earl said they're bound to be civil rights workers. Sam spotted the Jeep Wednesday night. Rayford—he saw 'em Thursday night, and Earl—he saw 'em last night. Earl said he tried his best to get close to 'em so he could get a good look. But the Jeep took off and he couldn't get close because of the dust."

Roger asked, "What color is it?"

Barney answered, "They say it's red."

Roger continued, "What kinda car tag does it have?"

Barney said, "They say it don't have no tag. That's another thing that makes it look suspicious."

Clawd summarized, "I'll be damn. A Jeep with no tag . . . being driven by white women nobody around here knows . . . spotted three different times out in the county. By God, I bet those two gals *are* civil rights workers. And I bet they're out there right now stirring up our niggers."

Alex opined, "My guess is they're nuns."

Barney suggested, "Or petticoat preachers."

Roger inquired, "You say they've been spotted three times?"

Barney explained, "That's what I heard this morning at the cattle sale. They've been spotted by old man McDonald, by Sam Porter, and by Rayford Pigott. Spotted each time at night between nine and ten o'clock out on Stringer Road.''

Alex asked, ''Where'bouts on Stringer Road?''

Barney answered, ''On the strip through the Okatala Swamp near old man McDonald's place.''

Alex mused, ''I'll be damn. Civil rights workers in Naboshuba County. I can't believe it.''

Roger said, ''Me neither.''

Alex continued, ''Like I said a few moments ago, the world's goin' straight to hell in a handbasket.''

Clawd inquired, ''You say they've been spotted between nine and ten o'clock the last three nights?''

Barney explained, ''That's right. On Stringer Road.''

Looking at his watch, Clawd proposed, ''I've got an idea. As many times as the four of us have coon hunted in Okatala Swamp, we know that strip of Stringer Road like the back of our hand. I'm gonna lock up and let's go out there and see if we can spot 'em.''

Barney added, ''And catch 'em and give 'em hell.''

Clawd commented, ''If we get our hands on 'em, we'll make 'em wish they'd never come down here to Naboshuba County.''

TEN

The Okatala Creek Bridge

PUTTING OUT THE LIGHTS, also turning off the air conditioner, Clawd locked the pool hall's door. Clawd, Alex, Roger, and Barney exited. The night air was hot and humid. The four men got into separate vehicles—Clawd and Roger into cars, Alex and Barney into pickups. Both pickups had gun racks holding twelve-gauge shotguns.

They pulled out of Honea Street, drove three-quarters around the square, and headed for the Sweet Pilgrim community. Stringer Road—their destination—made a loop from the Sweet Pilgrim community through the Okatala Swamp back to the south side of Clearwater. A gravel road, it was called "Stringer Road" because it passed through land which had constituted the pre-Civil-War Mason Stringer plantation.

The four vehicles, in tandem bumper to bumper,

made their way through the Sweet Pilgrim community. They passed the Sweet Pilgrim Baptist Church. One mile beyond the church they turned off onto Stringer Road.

A half-mile farther, Stringer Road entered the Okatala Swamp. It ran through the swamp for two miles. In the middle of this two-mile stretch was the Okatala Creek Bridge, a structure well known in Naboshuba County. Some 400 feet long, the Okatala Bridge had one lane set atop huge oak pilings taken from the surrounding swamp. Every Naboshuba Countian knew it was one-laned and had no railings. So everyone crossed the bridge gingerly. When you came to it, you had to stop and make certain no car or truck was crossing from the opposite direction. The bridge provided passage over low ground which was dry most of the year. But a bridge over this terrain was necessary, because in the rainy season (particularly during March and April) the Okatala Creek rose and flooded out of its channel, transforming adjacent lowlands into a marsh.

Arriving at the swamp's edge, Clawd pulled his car over to the roadside, got out, and motioned for the others to stop.

Responding to Clawd's signal, Roger, Alex, and Barney pulled their vehicles to the roadside, stopped, and got out. The four men stood in the middle of the gravel road. The night was pitch black. In the air were sounds of frogs and crickets.

Clawd said, "I believe in using my head for something besides a hat rack. So while I was drivin' out here I figured out a plan. If that Jeep comes through, let's hem it up on the Okatala Bridge. Here's how we can do it. Barney, you and Roger go on across the creek, drive about a quarter mile and park, headed back this way. Me and Alex, we'll stay here. If the Yankee women come through over there, let 'em by and follow 'em, blowing your horns. If me and Alex hear you blowing, we'll hustle to the bridge, blocking it this way. With you two behind 'em, we'll have 'em blocked on the bridge. If they come by us first, me and Alex'll start blowing and we'll follow 'em on the bridge while you and Roger block it from the other side. Either way—we'll have 'em hemmed up. They won't be able to go backward or forward."

Barney opined, "Sounds like a good plan to me."

Clawd continued, "We'll need shotguns just in case. You can't ever tell what might happen."

At this suggestion, Alex and Barney hustled to their pickups and removed from gun racks four loaded twelve-gauge shotguns. Alex handed one to Clawd and Barney handed one to Roger.

Wiping his gun barrel with his handkerchief, Alex quipped, "This twelve-gauge shotgun is gonna scare the shit out of them Yankee bitches."

Clawd, Roger, and Barney laughed.

Roger got into his car, and Barney hopped into his

pickup. They started their motors and headed down the road into the Okatala Swamp, their headlights piercing a darkness which was black as coal tar.

Clawd and Alex listened as the two vehicles, rattling the bridge's wooden boards, passed over the Okatala Creek. The sound of the motors died in the distance.

Clawd and Alex, lighting cigarettes, stood beside the road.

Moments passed.

Fifteen minutes slipped by.

A half-hour elapsed.

Alex said, "Bullshit, we're wasting our time."

Clawd responded, "Maybe not. Let's hang on. It's just nine-thirty."

Alex, with excitement said, "Be quiet! I think I hear a car comin' down the road."

Clawd said, "By God, I believe you're right!"

In the distance two vehicular horns began sounding.

Alex, with tenseness, exclaimed, "That's Roger and Barney honking. The Yankee bitches is comin'."

Clawd jumped into his car and Alex into his pickup. Turning ignition keys, they headed for the bridge. They drove to the middle of the span and turned off their headlights. Seizing shotguns, getting out, they stood on the bridge.

A vehicle, its headlights on, drove onto the span from the far end. It was being followed by a car and truck, both sounding their horns.

The vehicle drove to the middle. Being blocked by Clawd Fiker's car, it stopped. The vehicle, its motor now turned off, was a red Jeep. Two women were inside. They were Jesus and Simon Peter, both in the female forms they had assumed while visiting the Sweet Pilgrim Church and Lulabell's Lounge.

Clawd and Alex, carrying shotguns, walked up to the driver's side while Barney and Roger, also carrying shotguns, walked up to the other side.

Roger, in addition to a shotgun, was carrying a hunting light. He turned the light on and shined it in the women's faces.

Tauntingly, Roger said, "Well, I'll be, if it ain't two lady folks."

Clawd, also speaking sarcastically asked, "Where're you gals from? I bet you're from *Boston.*" He spoke the word "Boston" with a feigned Northern accent.

Clawd continued, "Or maybe from *Chicago.*" He uttered "Chicago" with a mock Northern brogue.

Giggling, Barney joined in. "Hey, Clawd, I bet they're nuns."

Roger continued shining the light on the women's faces.

Barney, grinning, remarked, "Or maybe they're petticoat preachers."

Alex joined the verbal humiliation. He said, "I got an idea. Maybe they're hymies."

Clawd said, "That's it. They're kikes."

Alex, speaking with acidity, said, "Are you gals kikes?"

The two women remained silent.

Roger remarked, "They ain't sayin' nothin'."

Mockingly, Clawd inquired, "Are you two lady folks too good—too high falutin'—to talk to us rednecks?"

Moments passed. The men's frustration grew.

Clawd instructed, "Barney, see what the tag says."

Barney answered, "It ain't got no tag."

Clawd, with rising anger, growled, "I wanta tell you kikes or nuns or petticoat preachers—or whatever the hell you are—that us folks in this part of the country got along just fine until you civil rights workers come down here from the North and started stirring things up. Trying to make us mix with the darkies. Trying to get the niggers to vote. And we're gettin' tired of it. And some of us are takin' it on ourselves to put a stop to it."

Clawd took his shotgun and poked its barrel into the Jeep.

He taunted, "You gals don't think I'll shoot, do you?"

The two women remained silent.

Losing his temper, Clawd exploded, *"Damn it, say something!"*

Simon Peter said, "Go to hell!"

Clawd, outraged, yelled, "Did you hear what that kike said? By God, you're not gonna get away with that! Barney, you and Alex and Roger step back!"

They responded to Clawd's command. Shotgun blasts

erupted in the night air. The faces of the women were savaged—mutilated beyond recognition. The women's blood splattered the vehicle's interior.

Clawd, breathing heavily, barked, "Let's push this goddamn thing in the creek."

Alex opened the Jeep's door, put the shift in neutral, and turned the front wheels sharply to the right.

The four men gave the Jeep a push. It rolled off the bridge and—with a loud, splashing noise—fell into the jet-black water of Okatala Creek.

All the men said, "Let's get our asses out of here!"

ELEVEN

The Discovery

THE JEEP, containing corpses, landed upside down in the water. It sank to the bottom, lodging against the bridge pilings. The water's depth was such that only the wheels were partly and barely visible. The rest of the Jeep was submerged.

Saturday night, Sunday morning, and Sunday noon passed. Several cars passed across the Okatala Creek Bridge, but no one noticed the almost completely submerged vehicle. Its proximity to the pilings took it out of easy view.

Rufus McKinley, seventy-one years old, physically spry, was a retired employee of the United States Forestry Service. For years, Rufus had driven out every Sunday afternoon from Clearwater in order to fish (weather permitting) in the Okatala Creek.

His Sunday routine never varied. Immediately after

his noon meal, Rufus took an early afternoon nap. Then he got in his car (an impeccably clean maroon Oldsmobile) and drove to the Okatala Creek Bridge. Parking his car on the roadside, Rufus would take his fishing gear and a canvas folding chair and walk down to the creek's edge. There he would fish for two or three hours. Whether or not he caught anything mattered little. Rufus enjoyed being out in the open, listening to the birds, watching squirrels scamper up and down trees, and looking at an occasional deer that came to drink out of the creek.

That Sunday afternoon in August, Rufus followed this routine. For an hour he sat in his canvas chair beside the Okatala Creek, idly fishing, puffing away on his pipe, waving to the occasional car which crossed over the bridge.

Rufus lazily looked at the stream flowing beneath the Okatala Bridge, some hundred feet away. Focusing his eyes, he looked again. The thought hit him that something strange was protruding from the water. Or something different. Whatever it was, it hadn't been there last Sunday.

Rufus, puzzled and curious, stood and made his way down the creek bank, edging closer to the bridge.

Rufus looked closely.

And then it dawned on him. He was looking at four partly visible automobile tires. That meant a submerged car was in the creek.

Rufus, feeling his heart beating faster, muttered, "My God!"

He dropped his fishing pole and started running toward the road.

Down the road toward the Okatala Bridge came three speeding cars, all filled with youngsters who were students at Clearwater High School. Out for a Sunday afternoon of jolly hell-raising, the youngsters were drag racing. They were racing down Stringer Road through Okatala Swamp and back to Clearwater. The first car, they had agreed, to get back to town and park behind Hinson's Texaco Station would be the winner.

Seeing the approaching cars, Rufus took out his handkerchief and started waving it in the air.

Recognizing Mr. Rufus—a man they all knew—the youngsters came to a stop.

Barry Stringer, driver of the first car, yelled, "Mr. Rufus, is there a problem?"

Mr. Rufus replied, "I've spotted a car in the creek!"

At those words, six automobile doors opened simultaneously. Eighteen high school students piled out. Excited, they followed Mr. Rufus to the middle of the bridge. They peered down into the creek and there it was. Lodged against the pilings. Undeniably, a submerged vehicle.

The girls screamed and closed their eyes.

The boys, showing pseudo-virility, cursed.

Mr. Rufus said, "You kids go back to town and get the

sheriff. I'll stay here. There may be somebody in that car. If there is, they're gonna be dead."

What had begun as a lark for jolly hell-raising was transformed into a mission. In thirty seconds, eighteen high school students dashed into three cars, reversed direction, and headed down the road toward Clearwater—all three cars blowing horns as though announcing the end of the world.

They drove to the police station and told Sid Stringer, who in turn called Bud Honea, the sheriff. Within minutes, Bud Honea, plus two members of Clearwater's three-man police department, plus the Clearwater Volunteer Fire Department, plus several cars filled with curious citizens, plus the cars with the high school students were headed for the Okatala Creek Bridge.

Arriving at the bridge, being shown the submerged car by Mr. Rufus, Bud Honea—the sheriff—realized he had a problem—a real problem—on his hands.

Various proposals were made.

"Let's get down there in the creek and see if we can turn it right side up."

"Can't do that. The water's too swift. And it's jammed against the pilings."

"Why don't we see if we can lift it up? Let's try to float it."

"That ain't gonna work. The water inside that car weighs a ton."

All proposed solutions, on analysis, seemed futile.

Sid Stringer, town policeman, proposed, "Let's call Jerry. Maybe he'll know what to do." The "Jerry" referred to was Jerry Amason, owner of Amason's Shell Station and Wrecker Service. Jerry had recently replaced his old wrecker with one mounted on a spanking-new GMC truck. Black in color, trimmed in gold, sporting on the cab a revolving orange light, this wrecker was Jerry's prized possession—the kind of wrecker he had always wanted to own.

Sheriff Honea called into town over his car radio. Working through Clearwater's police station, he called Jerry's home. No one answered. And so he called Addie Mae Steele, Jerry's married sister, to see if she knew where her brother was. Addie Mae told the sheriff that Jerry was right next door eating homemade ice cream with his in-laws. The fact was, she could see his car through her kitchen window. The sheriff told Addie Mae to go next door and tell Jerry that a car was under water at the Okatala Creek Bridge and for him to bring his wrecker out to the bridge as soon as he could.

The message was delivered, and twenty-five minutes later Jerry came driving up to the bridge in his new wrecker, its orange signal light whirling around and around.

Jerry got out of the wrecker and listened intently to what the sheriff and Mr. Rufus had to say. Surveying the situation, he walked up and down the middle of the bridge. He looked time and again at the submerged vehicle, pondered the current and the bridge's height, and noted the way the submerged car had been pushed by the current against the pilings. Never—in twenty-two years in the wrecker business—had he confronted a situation like this.

Jerry opined, "Bud, this ain't gonna be easy. Naugh, it's not!"

The sheriff, Jerry, Mr. Rufus, all members of the Clearwater Volunteer Fire Department, and dozens of bystanders fused their minds on one problem: what would be a feasible way to get the car out of the creek?

A plan was finally devised. Contact Vernon Pittman, owner of Pittman's Bulldozer Service. Get Vernon to bring out his bulldozer and clear a roadway straight to the creek's edge. In recent days, fortunately, it had not rained. Thus, the lowland, over which the roadway would run, was dry. After the strip had been cleared, Jerry could then back his wrecker to the creek's edge. A cable could be attached to the car, and it could then be pulled out.

This plan, everyone agreed, would take time. However, there was no other way.

By now it was five o'clock in the afternoon. But it was August, and days were long.

News of the accident had been reported over WNCC, Clearwater's radio station. This radio announcement, repeated several times, prompted scores of curiosity seekers to drive out to the accident scene.

Vernon Pittman was contacted. Vernon hauled his bulldozer to the site on a flatbed truck. He unloaded the bulldozer and—uprooting bushes, undergrowth, vines, and pine saplings—cleared a usable roadway from the road to the creek's edge.

This clearing operation took until almost eight o'clock. While people stood on the bridge and watched, Jerry backed his wrecker down the just-cleared strip. He backed it to the creek's edge. By this time a boat had been brought to the scene. Holding the end of the wrecker's cable, Jerry and Billy Wood, a member of the Clearwater Fire Department, paddled in a boat out to the sunken car. They attached the wrecker's steel cable to the axle.

Jerry and Billy then paddled back to the bank. Using skills acquired from over two decades in the wrecker business, Jerry—with his GMC motor sounding at times like a freight train—gingerly coaxed the vehicle away from the pilings. And then he pulled it through the water to the creek's edge.

Nightfall had arrived. Bystanders, holding flashlights and hunting lights, flooded the emerging vehicle with a sea of light. Adding to the illumination was the spotlight on Jerry's new wrecker. Jerry remarked, "This is the first time I've used that spotlight. It does a damn good job."

As the vehicle slowly emerged out of the Okatala Creek, the onlookers—now over three hundred in number—gasped.

Someone yelled, "It's a Jeep!"

"It sure is!"

As the Jeep was maneuvered onto the bank, water gushed out through its windows.

People shouted, "Is anybody in there?"

"We can't tell yet!"

"Let the water drain out!"

The Jeep, still upside down, was now completely out of the water and on dry land.

Bud Honea, holding a flashlight, looked inside the upturned car.

He yelled, "My God! Somebody's in there!"

A murmur reverberated through the crowd.

"Open the doors!"

"They won't open! They're jammed!"

"Has anybody got a crowbar?"

"Bud needs a crowbar!"

A crowbar, belonging to Vernon Pittman, was secured. Members of the Fire Department pried open the door on the driver's side.

"My lord, there's a woman in here!"

"A woman?"

"Yeah, a woman!"

"Two of 'em!"

"I can't believe this!"

"God almighty damn!"

The corpses were removed and were laid on the ground. Lights were focused on them.

"God almighty, what happened to these people?"

"They've been shot!"

"Their faces are gone! They're a bloody mess!"

By late Sunday night, practically every person in Naboshuba County knew that a red Jeep, lacking a license plate, had been pulled out of the water at the Okatala Creek Bridge. Two women, their faces mutilated with buckshot, were inside. Who they were or where they were from, no one knew.

Bud Honea, the sheriff, went home that night and vomited. For days he couldn't sleep. He told his wife, "Looking at them dead women's faces is the worst thing that ever happened to me."

TWELVE

"They've Shot Jesus and Simon Peter!"

LATE SUNDAY NIGHT, using his flatbed truck, Vernon Pittman hauled the Jeep into Clearwater. He parked his flatbed truck with the wrecked Jeep on it in front of the police station, opposite the courthouse.

Monday morning the townsfolk gathered around to gape. The Jeep's roof was caved in. The doors were ajar. The interior was soggy and muddy. The windshield was broken. Painted on each side was a Star of David.

People walked around the battered vehicle, asking questions, making cracks, expressing opinions. Disjointed conversations took place.

"They tell me Rufus McKinley found it."

"That's what they say."

"He spotted it stuck against the bridge."

"Where'd they take the bodies?"

"To the morgue in Vicksburg."

"I understand them women had been shot."

"That's right."

"Old man McDonald told the sheriff he heard shotgun blasts Saturday night about ten o'clock."

"He don't live too far from the bridge. I 'spect he did hear 'em."

The spectators continued circling the Jeep, looking, talking, speculating. While doing so, they squinted and smoked cigarettes and spat on the pavement.

"What in the world were two strange women doing out there in the Okatala Swamp that time of night?"

"Beats me."

"They'd been in the county a day or two. Sam Porter and Rayford Pigott swear they'd seen 'em."

"Who could they be?"

"The best guess I've heard is they were civil rights workers from up North."

"If that's so, they got what they deserved."

"Damn right they did."

"Any idea who done it?"

"Nobody's sayin'."

"Their faces were blown off. They looked like raw meat."

"I heard the sheriff say they couldn't find a credit card or a driver's license or a purse or nothing."

"That's weird. Really weird."

That Monday morning around ten o'clock Chester Travis, who on a rainy night had conversed with Jesus and Simon Peter at his honky-tonk, drove up from Catfish Landing to the courthouse to pay his taxes. He parked on the courthouse square.

Chester was one of the few persons in Naboshuba County who had not heard of the Okatala Bridge accident. Seeing a crowd gathered around the flatbed truck which was parked in front of the police station, curiosity filled, Chester ambled over to find out what was going on.

Hank Crawford, courthouse square loafer and tobacco chewer, assumed responsibility for telling Chester what had happened.

Hank launched into a recital of the events which transpired Sunday afternoon and evening at the Okatala Creek Bridge—about the Jeep's discovery, its removal from the water, and the recovery of two mutilated female corpses.

As Hank continued his account, he noticed Chester perspiring profusely. Chester became more and more agitated. Around Clearwater, Chester Travis had the reputation of being a dignified man, a solid citizen who minded his own business and ran a tight ship at Lulabell's Lounge. Not once had the police or the sheriff been called to break up a lounge fight. If trouble occurred, Chester took care of it.

Thus, the white people gaping at the battered Jeep

were nonplussed when Chester suddenly collapsed to the ground. He screamed at the top of his voice, *"Don't you white folks understand what they've done? They've shot Jesus and Simon Peter!"*

The whites stared at the screaming black man. They did not know what to make of Chester's anguished cry.

For a week, the corpses which were removed from the submerged Jeep remained in the Vicksburg morgue. Finally, unable to be identified, they were buried in paupers' graves in a cemetery to the east of the Vicksburg National Park.

THIRTEEN

"When the Saints Go Marching In"

SIX MONTHS had passed since that Easter Sunday in March on which The Sweet Pilgrim Miracle began. The last Sunday in September arrived—the Sunday on which the Sweet Pilgrim Baptist Church always observed homecoming. Across the years, these annual homecomings were festive occasions. Relatives who had "moved off" to Mobile, Memphis, and Jackson returned. Visiting quartets appeared. The Lollipop Ragtime Band regularly drove up from New Orleans. Smiles, laughs, slaps-on-the-back, handshakes, kisses, hugs, and food abounded. Adults greeted youngsters, "My, oh my, but how you've grown!" Adults greeted adults, "How good you look!"

But the 1964 homecoming—instead of being joyful—

began on a somber note. For weeks, news had circulated through the Sweet Pilgrim community about Jesus' and Simon Peter's fate at the Okatala Creek Bridge. Chester Travis, Rosco Jones, and Moses Stringer, the black men at Lulabell's Lounge on the rainy night when Jesus and Simon Peter visited this honky-tonk at Catfish Landing, had told the Sweet Pilgrim community about Jesus and Simon Peter coming that night to Lulabell's Lounge in a Jeep. They'd also told how Jesus, before leaving the lounge, had predicted Sam Bernsteiner's appearance.

People had said to Chester, "Maybe the Jeep they pulled out of the creek wasn't the same one Jesus and Simon Peter was in when they visited Lulabell's Lounge."

But Chester had responded, "Yes, it was. Miss Jesus' Jeep—like the one on Mr. Vernon's flatbed truck—was fiery red, and it had painted on the sides those funny-lookin' signs that look like triangles sittin' on top of each other."

Moreover, from community gossip the Sweet Pilgrim blacks learned that Jesus and Simon Peter had been shot in cold blood by rednecks from Clawd Fiker's Pool Hall. Reflecting on what had happened, they intuited that Jesus had appeared in their midst and had grappled with a fundamental problem—black exclusion from this country's economic mainstream. Jesus had provided them with a slice of the economic pie, and this they had never had before. But in doing so, Jesus, along with Simon Peter, was lynched at the Okatala Creek Bridge —a lynching rooted in racism, that bizarre form of moral evil which sanctions group sadism toward the innocent, the vulnerable, and those of different skin color. That is why the Sweet Pilgrim blacks said, "This old world has crucified Jesus again. A long time ago they done it at Calvary. Now they done it again at the Okatala Creek Bridge."

As the 1964 homecoming got underway, the Sweet Pilgrim sanctuary, as usual, was filled with parishioners and with visiting friends and relatives. Chester Travis, owner of Lulabell's Lounge, came out for the occasion. Alex, Sidney, and Roger Brumfield—the Lollipop Ragtime Band—drove up from New Orleans.

The service began with hymn singing. The names of those who had died since the previous homecoming were read, and a prayer was offered for their souls. A collection was gathered. Then Fishpole started reading a passage from the Bible. He was reading the parable about Lazarus and the rich man.

Aunt Mandy was the first person to hear the music. In the midst of Fishpole's Bible-reading, she abruptly stood, her always-erect bearing fired with a spirit of anticipation.

Interrupting, Aunt Mandy explained, "Fishpole, I hear the music! I hear the music again!"

Fishpole stopped reading.

Silence descended over the congregation.

Aunt Mandy was right. Sure enough—far off in the distance and coming again from the direction of the Mississippi River—was celestial music. Its volume grew louder as its source moved closer to the Sweet Pilgrim Baptist Church. The ethereal music engulfed the sanctuary and congregation. Simultaneously, the heavenly white cloud, emerging out of the floor, filled the building. The music and cloud, as upon previous occasions, conferred upon the parishioners feelings of serenity and joy. No one was afraid. Curiously, the supernatural event seemed natural to everyone in attendance.

The billowing cloud became so intense that no one could see the person sitting on either side. But then the cloud thinned. The evaporating cloud disclosed two beautiful and smiling women clothed in elegant dresses. Recognizing Jesus and Simon Peter, the congregation stood and cheered. They clapped their hands.

Parishioners shouted:

"That's Jesus and Simon Peter!"

"Hallelujah!"

"It's Easter all over again!"

"They done come back alive!"

The applauding and shouting continued until Jesus and Simon Peter beckoned for silence. The congregation quieted.

With smiles on their faces, waving their arms, Jesus and Simon Peter said, "Hello, everybody!"

The congregation returned the greeting.

From the rear of the sanctuary, someone yelled, "Those shotguns couldn't kill you, and the creek couldn't drown you!"

The parishioners laughed and cheered.

Fishpole asked, "Miss Jesus, this time can you and Simon Peter stay with us?"

Jesus answered, "Fishpole, we can't. We wanted to come back briefly to let you know we're alive and well in heaven."

Fishpole commented, "We sure wish you'd stay."

Jesus responded, "We can't. In fact, we must leave within the hour."

A disappointed murmur swept over the congregation.

Smiling, responding to the murmur, Jesus turned to the congregation and asked, "Would any of you like to go with us?"

Aunt Mandy exploded, *"I most definitely would!"*

Other voices joined in.

"Me, too!"

"I'd like to go!"

Fishpole, nonplussed, said, "Miss Jesus, do you mean what you're saying?"

Jesus answered, "I certainly do! I'm extending to everyone here today an invitation to go with me to a realm of joy and peace . . . to a place where people don't hurt one another and where all our needs are fulfilled."

Isaiah Brumfield spoke up and said, "Miss Jesus, we

108

all wants to go to heaven. Ain't no doubt about that, but I just bought me a brand-new Cadillac—the first Cadillac I ever owned—and I sho' hates to leave it. Could I by any chance take it with me?"

Jesus said, "Sure, you can. If you want to bring your Cadillac along, that's fine with me."

Jason Honea asked, "How about my new air-conditioned John Deere tractor?"

Jesus answered, "That's fine, too."

And then Jesus, speaking with enthusiasm, said, "Everyone who wants to go to heaven with me, go outside and get in line!"

A mass exodus took place. Piling out of the sanctuary, parishioners started getting into vehicles—new cars, new pickups, new tractors.

Going outside, Jesus gave instructions concerning the order for people to be in. At the front she placed Fishpole, Aunt Mandy, Tadpole, and the Lollipop Ragtime Band. The next person in line was Chester Travis. The rest of the congregation, all in their cars, pickups, and tractors, lined up—the caravan extending, it seemed, for a mile.

Jesus and Simon Peter then went to the front where Fishpole was standing. They turned to the Sweet Pilgrim congregants and called, "Are you ready?"

They answered, *"Yes! We're ready!"*

Jesus said, "Then follow me!"

Whereupon the Lollipop Ragtime Band, at Jesus' in-

109

struction, started playing "When the Saints Go March-ing In." The music produced by the Lollipop banjo, trombone, and trumpet was immediately comple-mented by cosmic music, so that the sky was filled with the melody of "When the Saints Go Marching In."

With Jesus leading, the line of vehicles began mov-ing. The front of the line started levitating. Defying grav-ity, the Sweet Pilgrim caravan began—at a gentle in-cline—moving into the air. Underneath the Sweet Pilgrim parade was a supporting roadway of mul-ticolored clouds. With Jesus and Simon Peter leading, the line moved higher. Fishpole was strutting. Aunt Mandy was cavorting. Tadpole was tap-dancing. The Lollipops were playing on banjo, trumpet, and trom-bone. Riding in vehicles, the Sweet Pilgrim congregants sang and laughed and waved.

The heavenly caravan passed over Clearwater right before twelve o'clock. In height, the caravan was just above the town's rooftops.

Seeing the caravan, becoming alarmed, Buck Brum-field, the officer on duty at the police station, sounded the community fire siren.

The siren's sound caused the churches in Clearwater to terminate immediately their morning services. Parish-ioners dashed out of the Baptist, Methodist, and Presby-terian churches. Looking upward, they saw the Sweet Pilgrim congregation moving through the air on a pave-ment of red and pink and yellow clouds. They saw

Fishpole strutting, Aunt Mandy cavorting, and Tadpole dancing. They heard the heavenly strains of "When the Saints Go Marching In."

Clawd Fiker, hearing the music, walked out of his pool hall. Looking upward, he also saw the heaven-bound caravan.

Chester Travis, operator of Lulabell's Lounge, recognized Clawd Fiker on the ground below. He called downward, "Hey, Mr. Clawd! You see those two ladies at the front? They're the two ladies you shot at the Okatala Creek Bridge! They're Jesus and Simon Peter!"

A disconcerted expression covered Clawd Fiker's face. Dropping the broom he was holding, he started running under the caravan.

Screaming, tears in his eyes, he called, "Jesus! I wouldn't have shot if I'd known it was you and Simon Peter. Honest, I wouldn't. But I didn't know! Nobody told me who you was!"

Clawd's screaming was drowned out by the melody of "When the Saints Go Marching In."

The Sweet Pilgrim congregation continued going upward, ever upward, traveling from Clearwater, Mississippi, toward heaven at Sunday noon.